Chilling Encounter

By Sam Grant

Published by Sam Grant

Publishing partner: Paragon Publishing, Rothersthorpe

ISBN 978-1-78222-685-7

Book design, layout and production management by Into Print
www.intoprint.net
+44 (0)1604 832149

Foreword

Action, mystery novel – *Chilling Encounter,* follows Mike Peters, who serves as first apprentice and then officer in the British Merchant Navy. A third, in a series, which begins with *Atlantic Hijack,* set in the nineteen-sixties. An era where there's a continuing rise in popular music and culture. The Beatles, are at Liverpool's Cavern club, for example, at the time depicted in the novel's main story.

In Chapter one of *Atlantic Hijack,* Mike Peters is a deck apprentice. *Chilling Encounter,* this novel, is a complete stand-alone story, where Mike Peters is offered a new position aboard the company Blue Circle Line's premier refrigerated cargo passenger liner, as that of Staff Captain. Individual novels track the career path of this fictional merchant navy seafarer.

In the prologue, to first action, mystery novel *Atlantic Hijack,* Mike Peters, is in the position of Second Mate, and about to sail aboard Ocean Melody for Buenos Aires and Rosario. Six years after the main story, beginning in chapter one, where he is a junior deck apprentice.

In Chapter one, Mike takes the reader back to when he was a junior apprentice aboard Albany Princess, leading into cargo liner Albany Princess's hijack in the South Atlantic. A varied cast of nautical character appear in this first in series, as the ship makes passage to South America.

River Escape, second in Sam Grant's action mystery series, revisits Mike when he is promoted to First Mate aboard *Albany Empress.* A ship bound from a lay-up in the river Fal, to a civil war outbreak in Venezuela. He is married, in *River Escape* with twin daughters Carol and Dinah. A stand-alone novel.

Novel *Chilling Encounter,* third in series, is a complete story, and begins, in chapter one with Mike, on leave from a ship which he has served aboard, as First Officer.

Former readers, will recall that Mike is not that keen on etiquette and social fraternising required aboard cargo passenger liners.

On leave, he is contacted by personnel and offered promotion from First Mate aboard a tanker to Staff Captain on Albany Contessa. Blue Circle Line's premier cargo passenger liner.

Chilling Encounter, similarly to first novel *Atlantic Hijack,* begins with a prologue. Mike Peters, in this prologue, is manager of a retail store in Plymouth. He experienced a leg injury, which has led to a change in occupation. Chapter one plunges the reader into the sea novel story when he is offered promotion, after *Albany Contessa's* Staff Captain is taken ill.

Premier passenger cargo liner *Albany Contessa* is to leave Liverpool, bound for Lagos with nine passengers and a valuable cargo aboard. Captain Pearce, the ship's captain has forgone the opportunity of taking his wife for a round voyage, this time and Mike's wife joins him, while the grandparents look after the twins, during the summer holiday.

Prologue

'Do make sure you give a full end to "lots 1351 and 2," suede accessories.'

It was Terri, buyer for leather goods, calling.

'The range is flying out in Marble Arch, Manchester and Liverpool.'

'Will do Terri, but they might not be as fashion conscious in the deep south west.'

'But you are a seasonal holiday hotspot Mr Peter's.'

'Not so hot. Preference is for a flight overseas to a week by the sea.' I admit that this comment was an attempt to cover my back if Terri's handbags, belts and gloves just didn't take off as anticipated in the sea port location of Plymouth.

'They'll be with your weekly Thursday delivery from Blatchers.'

'I'll look out for them Terri.'

'And I'll visit in a few weeks to update on buying strategy,' she said.

'Look forward to that. Bye for now.' I put the phone down.

Assistant manager Sarah arrived with a sheaf of sales figures.

'You know there's a staff meeting by the canteen entrance.' She smiled. Sarah performed the role of PA when considered necessary. Young enough to be my daughter. I appreciated her endeavours, to get me prepared for store events.

'You need to stress Mr Peters, that no one is to leave the store for stock except within their departments allotted rota time. And, that the dressing of counters and displays, from five onwards should not mean that the central till areas are left unmanned. Oh and there's this. A store night out to the Palace Theatre to see Diana Ross' Sarah placed a coloured theatre pamphlet on my desk.

'Will you be bringing your family?'

'They might be bringing me more like.' It was good to be included and not to seen as aloof and distant. The twins were near to that age when parents become a source of embarrassment. Uncannily though perhaps from my long absences earlier in their lives they still retained a proprietorial instinct to instruct and advise their father on shore life protocol. They would consider that I should attend a staff outing in my role as store manager.

Five years ago, and the idea that I would even have a position as store manager would have been dismissed. Although, my left leg was reassembled there was still a twinge whenever I moved from chair to feet. A chance meeting up with Duncan at the Wellington Arms was the point where I decided to change careers. Yes, there were opportunities for ex-merchant navy officers to teach at nautical colleges or to branch out into the administrative side of a shipping company or related port occupation. Port harbour master or maybe the Coastguard, but Duncan whom I met twice while ashore on study leave had now left sea life and was in retail. He was a buyer for a large store group and still travelled.

'They're crying out for managers. A new store's opening every month for the next year, he said when we met up at the Duke of Wellington.

'There's an initial training period. Then progress through to store manager. I was more interested in the buying side which came with travel and moved out of the stores,' he said

Retail trade is dependent on good business activity in the area. Basically, good levels of employment,' continued Duncan. I don't know about you Mike, but I felt that I wanted a change.'

'You made a conscious decision to leave the sea life. My crushed leg meant that I was no longer physically up to the mark.' I didn't mention that Jane decided that she wanted me to leave, even before the injury. I discussed the possibilities and whether she would be prepared to move out of Liverpool if need be.

'I've transferrable skills as a teacher you know,' she said. 'And Carol and Dinah will have their father at home.' After acceptance for initial training, I graduated through to store manager of first a store in Croydon. Now manager of the Plymouth store.

Certainly, as I stood to talk to staff and managers on the sales floor before the store opened

Five years previously I could not have envisaged this situation.

Chapter 1

It was unexpected. I'd not been that long on leave. Customarily there was no contact with Blue Circle Line once I was on the train back home. That is until near the end of leave.

'There's a Jeff Bridges on the phone.' Jane called me in, from the garden. I was, at that time, unaware that he was newly appointed, as personnel manager.

'Mr Peters?'

'That's me,' I replied.

'May I introduce myself?'

'Go ahead,' I said, not meaning to be facetious, but I expected this person to be probably an insurance company salesman or similar.

'Jeff Bridges, Personnel Manager, Blue Circle Line.' My tone changed to engaged and interested when I replied.

'Oh, right hello Jeff. You've replaced Bob.'

'Yes, he's wangled a transfer to the Buenos Aires office.'

'Lucky Bob,' I said. Although, I was happy to be settled with Jane and the twins back in the UK.

'Yes, that's my reaction. Sorry to interrupt your leave, Mike. Somethings cropped up. Well, I'll cut to the chase. Tim Burroughs has been taken ill, with a liver complaint. Don't know if you...'

'Yes, I do know, Tim's Staff Captain aboard Albany Contessa.'

'That's right. Appreciate that you're into your second week of leave, but Captain Watson asked if I'd give you a call.'

And that's how I found myself in the new suite of rooms adjacent to an insurance company's typing pool at Albany House, Liverpool. I knew that the fleet was much diminished from earlier days. Regular liner runs reduced or vessels scrapped. There were two new tankers added to the previous fleet of four, one of which I'd recently signed off.

The two of us, that's Captain Watson and myself, after first meeting, sat in a corner alcove away from the main office, and the office desk. Captain Watson was in the role of managing director, but retained his sea-going title.

'You'd have the same position, as Tim. We'd want you to take promotion to Captain for the duration of the trip Mike. Four cargo liners are now picking up cargoes like tramp steamers and tankers are reliant on charters from oil majors. John Bolton would turn in his grave if he knew the fleet was reduced to this! By the by, Contessa's due in at Liverpool, minus a Staff Captain.' Albany Contessa was one of two company refrigerated passenger cargo liners.

'Does that mean he's been DBS'd home, earlier or? (Distressed British Seaman)

'Yes, he was flown to the Royal hospital, after transfer first to a passenger liner, with a ships doctor.

'That's how it is and Contessa's back in port and due to sail next week.' It was Tuesday.

'Look Mike. Contessa's contracted to take machine parts and other manufactured goods outward bound to Nigeria and return with melons and cocoa. In a month's time when your leave ends, there's no guarantee there'll be a First Mate's position available. The way things are.'

'How much time have I got to decide? I mean I'll need to explain to Jane and the twins. Father and mother in-law are staying over.'

'How long's that for?'

'At least two months. Possibly three.'

'Right Mike. Give my regards to Captain Anderson. How are they? I was First Mate on Albany Heroine before he took up piloting duties.'

'They're well. They've sold on the share of the estancia and are on the lookout for a small holding over here.' The phone rang and the captain walked back to his desk.

'Yes Felicity.' There was a pause before Captain Watson, said,

'Go tell the accountant, the contract's to be extended a further six months on Contessa, and that I'll get back.' Another pause and,

'Yes, Felicity you were right to let me know he's called,' and replaced the receiver.

'Blue Circle arranges what's called a victualling deposit with Shell for each new contract. A down payment of fifty thousand pounds. This basically keeps things afloat.'

'Sounds pretty hairy,' I said.

'Don't believe it's any better for the likes of Cunard and P&O.'

'I wasn't planning of getting myself aboard a passenger liner or any liner, in particular,' I spoke out. Captain Watson, placed both hands on his desk, smiled and replied.

'You were never that keen, Mike, on, how shall I put it? Etiquette of the cargo passenger liner.' I tried to be circumspect when I answered.

'Lengthy cargo liner port stays could make me look forward to getting back to sea. Once I was married to Jane, it was tanker pay and accumulated leave that held appeal.' I wanted to keep the gate open. It was policy that deck officers were expected to serve on all types of company ship, but Captain Watson knew that my preference was to serve aboard tankers. He picked up a photo from the desk and walked back to the alcove, sat down and turned the photo toward where I was sat. It was a photo of Albany Contessa. A modern raked funnel, prominent midships accommodation, two lifeboats per side and everywhere above the black painted hull, gleamed white, even masts and derricks.

'I've a proposition to make Mike. Been in contact with Captain Pearce. He's generously prepared to forgo an opportunity to take his wife on the customary once a year voyage, should Jane like to accompany you.'

'That sounds attractive, sir, but depends on what Jane thinks. I'll need to get back to you on that one, if you don't mind.'

'Understand, that Mike. Can you let me know your answer by, tomorrow? Just phone in, and I'll be able to reassure Captain Pearce. Look Mike – he's served the company for nearly fifty years. Still a remarkably fit man for a sixty-four-year old, but we do now see the appointment of a staff captain as an insurance policy.

'How do you mean?' I asked.

It's considered that he's sharp enough to continue in the role. Should you have any doubts radio in and we'll get him to stand down. I personally would have had Captain Pearce take early retirement, but Antony Bolton, John's younger brother has okayed it.' I wasn't likely to make a comment – the same future might await me, but neither did I want a role akin to Fletcher Christian on the Bounty and be challenging Captain Pearce's authority.

'Has Captain Pearce been for a medical recently?' I asked.

'Yes, a physical, but there have been rumours that he's become forgetful. A woman passenger, apparently needed to twice remind him that she lived adjacent to the Bolton's estate.'

'Was she in hope of special treatment?'

'Well maybe, but there've been remarks from pilots about having to repeat themselves. He's keen to make one last trip. Look Mike, I've diplomatically suggested to him that whoever he has as Staff Captain, will if the need arises take control of decision making, should this be necessary. Basically, Mike, I want you to get on that bridge if weather conditions deteriorate with heavy seas, storm, poor visibility. Where, Captain Pearce takes over, on the bridge, and when a pilot is aboard, entering and leaving port. Got that?'

'Yes, but will I need head office authority?'

Only if he becomes obstructive. But look Mike this is unlikely.'

'The First, Second and Third Mate?'

'First Mate Bill Cooper has been appraised of the situation. I don't expect you to receive any opposition. That's should the need arise, which I hope doesn't.'

Chapter 2

It was all very sudden, but there was enthusiasm all round that Jane should take this opportunity of a sea voyage at the start of the summer school holiday. At the time I considered the opportunity to sail as staff Captain a very positive move. It would be on the record, that I'd established the position of Captain.

Father and mother-in-law were both keen for me and Jane to get away, as it turned out.

Carol said that she preferred that granny Natalia stayed to look after them, because her cooking was better than her mother's and she was also better at helping her with spoken French. It was Dinah who wasn't as keen, but a bribery of twice weekly riding lessons won her around fairly quickly.

'There's a swimming pool and deck golf or such like,' I said to Jane. I considered a good approach to encourage Jane. Everyone else was in bed, both twins and grand-parents.

'I'll take a suitcase full of books to read and in between I'll continue with my memoir.

A few weeks of restful living, before a new school term. Just what the doctor ordered. This time I won't be working my passage.'

'Nor will there be many other passengers. No guarantee that they'll not be other women on Board.

'A few more crew members than aboard Albany Princess. But more comfortable cabins.'

'Sounds okay to me.' It was all working out very well and I was able to phone back acceptance,'

'I'll send a letter with the details this evening. Appreciate your helping out this time Mike,' said Jeff Bridges.

Jane's father and mother were property viewing for the week. Natalia, Jane's mother phoned every evening and new appointments and visits, were quick to be transmitted. It worked in well. They, that's, Jane's parents had found a house, but since the sellers wanted to organize furniture storage, prior to an overseas move, it was agreed that Paul and Natalia would not move in until early autumn. Rather than live in a hotel, until then, they could live at – Hanover Gardens. I was able to phone once the decision was made to go. With a frenzy of activity, with regard to preparing clothes, reading material etc...to take on Jane's behalf. Apart from obtaining Captain's epaulettes from Rayners and sorting out a suitable uniform jacket to have new Captain's braid stitched on, my seagoing clobber, for the main, was already in a tin trunk. I was ready to go. School summer holidays started a week previously and an opportunity for Jane and I to have a few weeks together was unlikely to occur again in the near future.

It was difficult to tell who were most relieved when Gran and Grandad returned from house hunting. Carol and Dinah or me and Jane. Our plans for joining Albany Contessa meant that interest shown toward our daughters' lives, just at that moment, was not getting the attention that they knew would be received from their grandparents. Both Natalia and Paul were experts around horses and were totally on Dinah's wavelength. Carol was the more studious of the two and had a summer project from school, which Natalia could assist with. It wasn't that Jane wouldn't have been involved, but one generation remove can lead to more tolerance between child and adult. Both, as twins, at an age where parents were seen as out of touch with the modern world they met with, although strangely their grandparents were not seen to be, as out of touch! Perhaps, because they were more willing to listen and to be less critical. Where, we as parents might place restrictions and not show interest in spheres that their grandparents would. Abilities, they might be able to develop beyond the skill of their mother and father. Almost like another schooling experience – albeit in the summer holidays.

'Do you remember this?' Jane produced a faded denim cap.' We were packing the day before departure.

'I do. You don't mean to say you've kept that cap all these years?'

'Yes, look.' Jane turned the cap to one side. There was a smudge of white paint across one side.

'As I reached inside the paint locker, it caught on the roof.' Jane pointed out the mark on the cap.

'I kept it to remind me of the trip.'

'Not of me?'

'That came later. I actually missed not being aboard the ship for quite some time after. And yes, Mike the cap became part of our relationship, you could say. It's a good luck talisman.'

I wasn't to upset for not being a first consideration. We were apart for several years before we met up again in Rosario, after all.

'Don't look put out, Mike,' she said.

'I'm not really.'

'This trip will bring back memories, though, from that first time.'

'Not bad ones, I hope.'

'You mean the hijack and how they killed Leckie?'

'We, were all shocked by that Mike. His death, was from a heroic act. We were all just caught up in their total disregard for others outside their cause.'

'I'm glad you see it like that.'

'I do.' Neither of us had talked overmuch about those traumatic days aboard Albany Princess, and I guess thoughts of returning to be together, aboard a ship brought them back again. We heard voices downstairs and then Natalia, Jane's mum called up.

'Are they old enough to see Raiders of the Lost Ark, Jane?' The strict father in me said earlier that perhaps the story might be too adult for them. As is ever the case, this fuelled the twin's enthusiasm to see the film, even further. Where my reservations resulted in a negative response, this was not the case, evidently with their grandparents Natalia and Paul Anderson.

'It's a PG mum. Up to you, if you want to take them, said Jane.' That was me overruled.

'Okay love, it's just that we're lining up some treats.'

'Treats, so long as they behave, I hope you mean?' Said Jane. 'I'll be down in a moment to help with tea.' We'd arrived at that point where being with the family took priority over all else now with the prospect of a number of weeks away at sea.

I followed Jane downstairs, and found that Carol and Dinah were about to leave with their grandfather to go to the shops.

'You're not to buy anything except what's on the list,' said Jane, knowing how her father was liable to buy treats. I wasn't sure how this was going to be checked out on, once Jane wasn't around, but her mother seemed to have been there.

'No, it's alright Jane. I've already sorted that.' Although teenagers, their grandparents seemed to be acceptable and not a cause of acute embarrassment, in quite the same way they found, when with us

'We're just glad to get away from mother and her packing,' said Carol. Grandad Anderson, made a wry face, as if to absolve himself from understanding what she meant.

'Come on you two, said Dinah, who appeared in the kitchen dressed in anorak and as keen as her sister to escape from the turmoil, as they saw it, of their mother's preparation for our departure tomorrow. It was probably, as well, in hindsight, that neither were to upset about not having their parents around and testimony to the bond that they already had with grandparents Natalia and Paul Anderson. We both sent photos and letters over the years

Although, there was the inevitable delay in receiving replies this was a dream come true for the twins that grandparents, who they only knew properly about through correspondence back here, in the UK. This, in spite of Dinah's dream being dashed, in that she said that she's always wanted to ride a horse across the Argentinean pampas.

A taxi was ordered for eight thirty. We breakfasted at eight. It was not the first time that we'd gone out together and left the twins with their grandparents and Natalia was up before we left, and said,

'Let them sleep. You said that you were leaving early.' We'd said our goodbyes, to Dinah and Carol before when they went to bed. They didn't seem that bothered, and told their mother to bring them something back. But you never know with teenagers, whether they're just putting on a brave face. Paul Anderson made an appearance in his dressing gown, when we were finishing our coffees. He sat in the chair by the fireplace. 'You've made the right decision. These are difficult times. I well remember during bad times, once signed on as an AB, just to get work. There were four of us with Masters Certificates. They were hard times. Just hope Mike that you don't have to go through anything like that.'

'Yes, there's definitely a down turn. It was either continuing on leave or taking this position aboard Contessa.'

'You've likely taken the right decision, Mike,' he replied. Natalia, walked through from the kitchen,

'Wish we could all go, but the twins will be alright here with us,' she said. It's not that long and you'll be back here soon Jane, anyway.' Our cases were in the hallway ready and not long after we were waving goodbye to not only Natalia and Paul, but the twins appeared, after all and the four stood together to see us off.

Chapter 3 (Liverpool)

I remember there being a light drizzle, but not enough to need raincoats or protection. Wipers, on the taxi barely needed when we started, but it was more overcast in the dock area. I always retained clear memory of first arrival to board a ship in the UK. Albany Contessa was moored well into the dock and became visible in front of a warehouse as we approached. At first funnel, white superstructure masts and lowered derricks were clearly visible from the taxi, but disappeared with only the black hull and railings clearly visible, as the taxi drew closer.

'Won't know myself aboard Albany Contessa, as a passenger,' said Jane, as the taxi drew to a halt on the far side of a tracked crane line. The driver turned to where we were sat on the back seat.

'It's alright gov. I've got a handy little truck that'll take your luggage to the gangway.'

'Are they expecting you? I mean to assist?'

'Don't know. We'll soon find out.' Unfazed by my reply, he said,

'Stay there while I load up, gov, missus. No need to stand in the rain longer than you have to.' He got out and opened the boot. We'd decided on three large suitcases. These were loaded on to a small expanding type of sack truck. Jane had a hand suitcase in the back, plus two carriers, one of which contained pot plants which were near to bloom. "Don't know whether they'll like the tropics, have to wait and see.'

'It'll be more whether they like the air conditioning,' was my reply. It would be novel having plants in the cabin. A tap on the window, followed by the door being opened by the driver to allow Jane to get out led into my question of 'How much do I owe you?' I gave a sizeable tip, on the basis that he was both friendly and resourceful.

'Thanks, gov, appreciated, and where you bound might I ask?' Jane answered.

'It's Lagos.'

'You'll soon be well clear of all this then. Not just the weather.' I guess he meant the sense that job prospects were not good in the area. I carried Jane's suitcase as the driver manoeuvred his truck across the crane track lines to the foot of the gangway. We stood at the foot, which was at a comfortable angle to walk up. Water discharge cascaded from an outlet near the stern and the throb of a generator deep in the bowels of the ship acquainted us with the ship's presence. That is apart from the black riveted hull which loomed up before us. By this time the taxi driver had unloaded the cases at the foot of the gangway and was making his way back to his car.

'Mr Mate, Mr Mate.' A familiar voice that of Joe Blackburn called from above. A sailor from aboard Ocean Melody. Then an EDH, now an AB, I was soon to be made aware of.

'I'll be down there. Here.' He appeared to wave and beckon to someone else.

'Come and give Mr Peters a hand with his clobber.' Not sure Jane would consider her belongings as in that category.

Two pairs of feet were soon clattering their way down to the dock where we were standing.

'Didn't expect to see you aboard one of these. Beg your pardon Missus? Were Joe's first words.

'My wife.' I explained, 'Will be aboard for this trip.' Joe considered this for a moment before coming back with.

'Then you're Captain, sir?'

'Staff Captain.'

'Same difference, ain't it? Hey Scaramouche grab hold of Mr – Captain Peter's and his missus suit cases. We'll see to these for you. You go on up sir, mam, we'll be right behind with these.' Scaramouche was the deck boy. Joe would likely address others in this way and it wasn't meant in an intimidating or bullying manner. I later found out that not only was I a replacement, but there were additional crew members signed on. Joe was on the company's books and moved around Blue Circle Lines fleet of ships.

Albany Contessa was at the time one of the premier ships in the fleet and I was familiar with the layout from serving aboard a sister ship way back when Third Mate. Both Captain and staff Captain quarters were adjacent to one another, on the same deck, with windows that faced the foredeck within the passenger accommodation. Three tiered decks, which accommodated passengers and senior offices on the uppermost deck, with First, Second, Third Mate plus engineers and electricians on the next one down; followed by an extended deck accommodation housing, which berthed, deck crew, boilermen, cooks and stewards.

'This is a big step up from Albany Princess,' said Jane. We'd climbed outer companionways to arrive on the awninged passenger deck. We walked along the deck marked out for deck golf and through a door into the accommodation. The Second Steward was in the corridor stood by an open linen locker, with folded sheets across an arm. I introduced myself and Jane.

'Captain Pearce has company, but I'll let him know that you're on board, sir. I've a key to your quarters and can let you in.' There was a clatter as the door we'd entered was flung open.

Joe came through and shouted back.

'You pass them through. Enough stuff to sink a battleship.'

Realizing, that we might be in earshot, Joe made to dismiss his comment with,

'Good journey Mr – Captain Peters, sir?'

'I can manage if you leave the cases in the corridor,' I said – 'thanks for the help.'

'That's alright. Good to have you aboard Captain.' When

we were alone in the cabin, Jane asked about Joe.

'Your fame spreads before you Mike, then?'

'You mean Joe? We go back to Ocean Melody days.'

'Then, he likely remembers our meeting in Rosario, when I came aboard with my class?'

'Most probably. There's not much gets past below decks with regard to who's who.'

'That's an awful long time ago, yet somehow it seems like yesterday.'

'It does,' I said. 'Could be a sign of getting old.'

'You said that not me,' said Jane. 'I don't feel any older than when we were aboard Albany Princess. I would have stayed around if I'd known you better then.' 'Hey.' Jane pulled back the curtains that covered forward facing curtains from one of two windows. 'That's a great view out there. Jane was in a side cabin before. What's that they're loading?'

I walked across and stood next to Jane. A pallet of cartons, swung across and hovered above Number two hold.

'It won't be chilled goods, probably spirits for a Nigerian Embassy, I wouldn't doubt. I'll need to get a look at the manifest. There's unlikely to be a full cargo outward bound. Jane said, out of the blue.

'I'm not the only woman, aboard, am I?'

'Have to wait and see. You might be.' This question was answered when there was knock on the door, which opened to reveal a stewardess with a tray of tea and biscuits. News of our boarding must have spread.

'Welcome aboard, Captain Peters and Mrs Peters. Angie's my name. Chief Steward sends his compliments and that Captain Pearce would like to see just you sir, in his cabin with the First officer, at five. We're due to leave tomorrow.'

'Yes, I'm aware of that.' Jane softened the abrupt entrance with,

'Thank you, Angie. That's something I've been looking

forward to,' directing attention to the tray with teapot cups, saucers and plate of biscuits placed on the table and turned to leave.

'Just leave the tray outside will you, when you've finished. We're all locked up in port.'

'Oh Angie, by the way,' I asked, who is the Chief Steward. I mean what's his name? Angie turned back from the opened door.

'The Chief Steward's Peter Haynes.' Her smile suggested that she was pleased about this, as indeed both Jane and I were. At least we knew one other person, apart from Joe aboard Albany Contessa. I'd not sailed with Peter since, the days of Albany Empress and apart from explaining the trauma of civil war and escape from the Orinoco I'd not made mention of Kimi, but felt that I could trust Peter not to spill the beans. The fact, that I'd got close to another Captain's daughter!

'The Chief did say that you'd met before. I forgot,' she smiled. 'He said to send his kind regards and can he visit before you meet with the captain?' It was a good job that I'd asked or we might not have been given Peter's message.

'Yes, that's fine,' I replied.

We'd finished drinking tea and eating biscuits with the tray, outside the door; Jane well forwards with unpacking when I recognized Peter's voice outside. He was calling out for a steward to collect the tray. Passenger cabin doors were open when we arrived, although they had yet to arrive. A polite tap on the door, followed.

'Mike, Jane, so good to see you.' A bearded Peter greeted us. His hair, like mine receded and was compensated, you might say with a white flecked dark beard. We shook hands. Jane shut the wall cabinet and walked over to where we were.

'Hello, Peter. A nice surprise.'

'Good to see you both again. And as a passenger this time Jane.

22

'It's a long time ago now Peter. Mike told me; you both were aboard Albany Empress.'

'Yes, that was a bit hairy, as I remember.'

'Wife and family – all well Peter?' I asked.

'Divorced, but it was amicable. It still is.' Jane continued.

'We've the twins, Carol and Dinah,' said Jane. They're at an age when they're quite keen to have their parents away for a while.

'Jane's mum and dad are back from Rosario and house hunting,' I came in with.'

'Your father the best Captain I've served under, Jane – save your husband that is.' He winked at Jane.

'Keeping fit is he – and Natalia?'

'Both very well, considering their age. Pleased that they're back in the UK, though.

'Look Mike I'm on my way down to the gangway to greet the passengers.' He looked at his watch.

'Ten to five,' he said. 'The agent's phoned to say they're expected by five.'

'We're to meet with Captain Pearce.' There was a momentary pause.

'Glad you're aboard Mike. Speak with you both later. Bye for now,' and Peter left us.

Chapter 4

I was familiar with Albany Contessa from a stint relieving aboard, while the ship was between ports, before the regular crew returned from leave. I knew of Captain Pearce and that he was like me a company's man, but unlike myself, his career had been aboard liners similar to Albany Contessa. Rumour, universal around the company, was that having married into the Bolton family, in that he married a cousin of the company's founder John Bolton, he could choose to stay serving, initially, but latterly captaining this refrigerated type of vessel. An awareness that Captain Douglas Pearce or, Dougie was connected to the powers that be, was daunting, for all of Captain Watson's suggestion that I should keep a watch on Dougie, like some kind of shipboard minder!

'Are you okay. I mean left here,' I said. It was twenty to five. There'd been no activity in the corridor outside. Captain Pearce, I assumed was in his cabin on the opposite side.

'What do you think? I'm a big girl,' Jane said. I'm happy to blend in as a passenger. I'm really curious to meet the other passengers.'

'From my experience they could be a motley crew,' I said, 'made up of company office people or ex-pats who enjoy British nationality but don't have much good to say about the old country.'

'It's a good job then that I'm with you to help prevent your prejudices getting the better of you then Captain Peters.' Jane was most likely right.

'You're not going like that are you? Jane asked.

'I was,' I said.

'Your uniform, shirt and tie are laid on the bed. It's a good job I'm here to make you aware that this is the Contessa you're aboard and Mike you're on a level with Captain Pearce.'

I'd not mentioned to Jane how Captain Watson expected

me to keep a weather eye on Dougie, but I conceded that she was right. Captain Pearce and the First Mate, Bill Cooper, would be in uniform, I needed to step up to the mark. All the life's a stage – that oft quoted Shakespearean line can be ascribed to the donning of a uniform. It's that life imitating art moment when you cannot help considering that police television dramas must to an extent influence not only real police behaviour, but also the public's imagination of what they expect police to be like. That a particular uniform imbues its wearer with an expected demeanour. Each position aboard a ship arrived at will be from watching and experiencing others in a similar role, whilst climbing that greasy pole upwards, as with all walks of life.

I walked from our cabin through a door which separated passenger accommodation and our cabin from, you would call the executive arm of the ship. Passenger accommodation was hived off from the officer's accommodation, save for the Staff Captain's cabin which matched Captain Pearce's cabin, save that Jane and I were on the port side, looking forward and the ship's Captain was on the starboard side. Twin corridors, bulkhead partitioned for port and starboard with mid door access. The Chief engineer's cabin was similar to Captain Pearce's, but faced the after deck, whereas the ship's Captain's cabin faced forward. Aboard tankers and other ships within the company, terminology of Mate, Second and Third Mate was common parlance, but aboard Albany Contessa, with passenger quotient there was a step change to now, Chief, Second and Third Officer on cabin doors. I would need to use this title when talking with passengers, I remember considering at the time. Just as I was mentally preparing myself to meet with Captain Pearce the deck access door opened and a tall boiler suited figure, crouched to enter. His first words were,

'Welcome, it's good to have you aboard.' His hand cold,

when we shook. from time on deck.

'Bill Cooper – Mate. You're replacing Tim?' Which was to state the obvious.

I liked the direct manner of Bill. We'd never met, but knew from Captain Watson that he had a similar background of serving on a mix of ship types.

'That's right. Mike Peters.' Out of nowhere he said,

Captain Pearce, Dougie can have lapses in concentration, you know.'

'That there are memory lapses. You need to check out decisions for yourself. I've taken to bridge duties in and out of port, since Tim left. No doubting that he had a liver problem, but arrived, in my opinion, from stress induced drinking.' He paused.

'It's difficult updating Dougie when you know he only partly remembers past events.' It was sounding that Dougie's condition was more dire than Captain Watson had made out. What about the passengers?' I asked.

'That's the surprising thing, he can hold conversations and appears his old self, you could say in the saloon.'

'But on the bridge, I mean ...?'

'You need to step in, particularly when the pilots aboard. I found it difficult, because, well,' he lifted his right arm and reached across to touch the sleeve of the boiler suit –

'With just the three bands,' I'm First Mate and not Captain.'

'Right,' I said. Bill continued.

'You're deputy, Mike as Staff Captain. Tim told me that he always made a point of making the pilot or pilot's aware of the situation. It worked because Sam Bates, the present pilot, knew Tim. He's due to board shortly, for departure, as I understand.'

'That's good then,' I said.

'Yes, Look. Shall I go in first? I mean... you do understand

Mike, that you are Captain of Albany Contessa, not deputy, as it appears. You have my backing.'

'Good to hear, in one sense,' I said. My pay, might not reflect the responsibility.' Bill smiled,

'What about me then?' There was always that standing joke about being well fed aboard these part passenger liners, but under paid.

'I've had to step up rank, in responsibility,' he smilingly replied, before he knocked on Captain Pearce's door and waited for a response, which was,

'Yes, you can take the tray,' expecting the steward. Bill opened the door.

'Captain Perace, cargoes near completion and we've got our replacement for Captain Burroughs.' In much the same tone of voice as he would address the steward, he replied,

'Well show him in, then.' Bill stood aside and I walked in. Captain Pearce was stood by one of two forward looking windows, without uniform jacket. He wore a blue V necked pullover, which would be hidden by the jacket, when worn. In one hand he held, what I soon learned was a passenger list. His first words were –

'And where's your wife?' Captain Pearce, aged sixty-four, was wiry for his age, with lined, almost mahogany face.

'In my cabin,' I explained.

'Right, we've nine passengers due aboard and with your wife I'm hoping we can assist with welcoming them. She'll be up for doing that?'

'Yes, I expect so,' I replied. Bill who was by the door said,

'Do you want me to ask?' He half whispered to me – your wife, Jane, isn't it?'

'No, I'll ask her myself, Bill. Jane will of course, be wanting to mix and get on with the passengers, as we all will.' I turned back and smiled I hoped, agreeably. This meeting, it seemed, wasn't starting too well, but I learnt that Captain Pearce did have mood swings and surprisingly, although experienced with having passengers aboard, was not as confident socially, as might be expected. There was no obligation for Jane to take on the role of passenger hostess. I wasn't entirely taken aback by my reception. Captain Pearce was a senior Master with direct owner association, through marriage, to a cousin. I was newly appointed and my background ship management experience was not mainly in cargo passenger liners. Certainly not, from lengthy service aboard, as prestigious a vessel as the Contessa.

'You appreciate, Captain Peters that your duties will be, in part, to ensure that our nine passengers are well catered for. That was a reason why we considered having your wife aboard. Might assist in getting you acclimatized to a role which requires more civilities than that expected aboard an oil tanker or bulk carrier, you understand.' A remark, which could have been seen as rude, but I would be first to admit that I preferred a role that required a boiler suit, more than that of uniformed flunky, with matched performance that pleased an audience of passengers. Didn't mention this, of course! At the time I was very fortunate to have made promotion in difficult ship trading weather, so to speak.

'Captain Pearce,' Bill's work gloved hands held the door frame on either side, whilst I was in the inner sanctum, you could say. He repeated himself.

'Captain Pearce, cargo works near complete. Peter, I mean the Chief Steward will shortly be seeing to the passengers and I'll be getting the crowd out on deck for departure, if that's alright?

'Yes, carry on Mr Cooper.' I kind of liked the way Bill turned back, once into the corridor gave a smile, and saluted, out of sight of Captain Pearce.

'Shut the door, Captain Peters. Mr Cooper's a capable Mate. Gets the best out of the crew.' Captain Pearce, kept a strict formality with regard to names and rank, I recall. But it was good to hear recommendation for Bill. A First Mate, could be a kind of whipping boy, who gets blamed for certain arduous work, which likely was actioned by the ship's Captain and not him. It appeared then, that Bill was though, on favourable terms with Contessa's crew.

'So!' Captain Pearce seemed to be making that assessment we can all be prone to on first meeting with another. Whether we like or dislike? His faced portrayed nothing to establish either way.

'This is your first appointment as Staff Captain?'

'Yes, came out of the blue with Tim being taken ill.'

'Burroughs worried unnecessarily and now it looks like he had a drink problem.'

'Really?' I replied innocently.

'Liver complaints are alcohol related, aren't they?'

'Not necessarily. I mean was he the worst for wear, at times? Did you have to step in?'

'No, but my impression was that the role stressed him and that would likely lead into excess drinking. That's my opinion Peters, and there it is.' Captain Pearce returned to look at the passenger list, before he began to read from it.

'John Palmerston-Smyth. Head office Johnny – on a sabbatical.

'You know him?' I asked.

'No, never met him. Something to do with estate management, apparently.

Daniel Musgrove and Helen Taylor. They're dual nationality. Returning to their home in Lagos, apparently.

Doctor and Mrs Lucy Sinclair. Assume that to be a medical doctor. Ah, here's a regular, Miss Jacqueline Braithwaite, retired head teacher. Has connections with the family.'

'You do know her then?'

'From previous trips. She usually ends up running a library

service; number of books she brings. A trunk full, usually. Never had such a well-read crew Peters, once she's completed a round trip.' Captain Pearce continued to read from the passenger list, whilst I experienced a feeling of wanting to be back aboard an oil tanker

Mr Stewart Hopkins and a Mr Paul Jenson. They've connection, with Blue Circle, oil contracts. Possibly being given a free passage back to Lagos.

Craig Hooper. Just says financial representative to shipper and of potential assistance to company, whatever that means?'

'Captain Watson mentioned that the company's running on bank loans.'

'Watson, is not exactly at the coal face. He's told what he needs to know.' Captain Pearce paused before continuing.

'Blue Circle Line, has ownership of more than just ships' Captain Peters.' I was given a return curtesy of Captain, where Captain Watson lost his.

'Right,' I said.

'I usually get a run through from Personnel about passengers. It's very much on a need-to-know basis and this time they must have considered there was nothing I needed particularly to know about. No special menus, disabilities or conditions, political points of view to be wary of.'

'You're informed about passenger's political views then Captain Pearce?'

'Yes, any situation, where there might be conflict of political opinion and you know as well as I do Peters, that British values of democracy don't register as relevant neces-sarily in the countries traded with, nor the passengers who travel aboard company ships. Steer away from ever having a political opinion one way or another. You'll appreciate that old saying, avoid talk about sex, politics or religion. Never more appropriate than when passengers sit with us in the dining saloon or when they're invited on to the bridge, for example.' A discrete knock on the captain's door followed. When opened revealed Chief Steward, Peter Haynes.

'Captain Pearce, the Second Steward's presently with the passengers in the officers Smoking Room.'

'All aboard then are they Chief?' I caught a glimpse of Jane who was stood just behind. She gave a small wave.

'Yes, Captain Peter's wife Jane is here Captain.'

'Well stand aside.' Peter, stepped aside, to allow Jane through.

'Jane, welcome aboard. It's really delightful to have you aboard. We're about to meet the passengers. Thrown in at the deep end. I do apologise, my dear, do come in, won't you?' Like a sun break through clouds to lighten all around, Captain Pearce's somewhat gruff demeanour became transformed, with Jane's arrival. Now changed into a dark blue suit, which I remember she'd worn, on occasion at school parent meetings. Business like, rather than glamorous. It seemed very appropriate on this occasion. She'd made a decision to be involved with the social side of meeting with the passengers, without my asking.

'Not a problem Captain Pearce. Really appreciate the opportunity to be with Mike and aboard the Contessa. Very excited about meeting up with other passengers.'

'Do hope you won't be disappointed with who we have aboard.' Jane replied,

'I'm sure they'll all be interesting company in their individual ways.'

'A very diplomatic reply. I can see that I will value having you on board.

Captain Pearce shook Jane's hand and placed his other one gently on her arm.

'Mike's a very lucky man.' Jane smiled. He let hold and walked across to pick up his cap, positioned on the top of his desk.

'I wear my cap on arrival, at Passengers lounge, but not you Peters. Passengers can find the idea of two captains a bit confusing, you understand.'

'Quite,' I said. 'Best to make things clear.'

'I'll lead the way then,' Captain Pearce, said. Peter conveniently had all the decks cabin keys, located on a very large key ring and just as he locked the captain's cabin to follow the three of us, Captain Pearce said,

'Inform, Mr Cooper that we're leaving in an hour's time and for him have the crew at stations, Chief Steward, will you.'

Chapter 5

Up until that moment when Captain Pearce mentioned to Peter about notifying Bill, that we were leaving, there was no real indication of memory loss. Evidently though, short term memory was an issue. It could be said that someone should have taken action and referred Captain Pearce to a doctor. Was his wife unaware? It's a difficult situation to face and maybe Captain Pearce, was hiding away from reality. He had been quick to resolve Tim Burroughs liver disease as caused by alcohol consumption. A convenient narrative for him, at the time.

After we followed Captain Pearce down the inner stairway to the next deck, he stopped.

'Oh, yes, he said we have soft drinks, when offered. That doesn't mean you, of course Jane. There, can be that drinking and driving thing on ships', particularly when leaving port.' This was news to me at the time.

'A ship's captain is on the bridge to steer the ship, can be the understanding for certain passengers. It's a very old joke. Burroughs was never keen on this rule before departure.'

I could hear chatter and activity from the Dining |Saloon several cabin doors away, past the passengers' lounge, when the Second Mate's cabin door flew open ahead of us. It would likely have been a busy time getting charts sorted, amidst the finalization of cargo stowage and he was fitting in a meal, while time allowed.

'Second Mate.' Captain Pearce called to him. He turned whilst buttoning his uniform jacket.

'Yes Captain.'

'Our new Staff Captain, Captain Peters and his wife Jane.' Bob Mitchel was red haired, freckled faced, mid-twenties, with an athleticism about him, which I could no longer make claim to.

'Pleased to meet you sir, and Mrs Peters.' Jane didn't hesitate, 'it's alright Second, I'd prefer to be on first names...'

'Bob, Bob Mitchel' replied the Second, with a smile.

'Not so you Captain Peters, though' interposed Captain Pearce.

'Good to meet you Bob,' I hastily said with,

'Like to get up on the bridge for ten minutes with you before we sail. That's before stations. Of course, after we've met with the passengers, sir,' I said to Captain Pearce.

'Won't be long in there,' said the Second. Should, be on the bridge straight after. That's fine, with me, Captain Peters,' said Bob, who continued his walk, past the Smoke Room, and toward the Dining Saloon.

I found it all a bit much, but ritual tribe that we are, the Second Steward was just inside the Smoke Room door. Captain Pearce's, capped arrival on the threshold, so to speak, led to a still in conversation. Women passengers, to be expected, were seated but men standing.

On entry, Captain removed his cap and handed it to the Second Steward. This presumably a ritual performance developed over time.

'Welcome aboard Albany Contessa, to everyone, on behalf of Blue Circle Line. Please continue. Chief Steward Haynes will shortly be here to make introductions.' Second Steward Patrick Donalds, meanwhile, had walked across to the bar and returned with a tray of wine glasses. Three quarters full, with variously orange, lemon and pineapple juice. Captain Pearce, turned toward Jane.

'You are not restricted, my dear. Would you prefer...

'No Captain Pearce I'll join the teetotal club, at this point. Quite happy with a soft drink.'

'Thank you Second,' she said and selected a wine glass of orange juice; Captain Pearce and myself followed, before I heard,

'Am I seeing double – two Captains. Double coverage, that's reassuring. May I introduce myself.' A man, in his forties, dressed, in light leather jacket, grey trousers and yellow roll top sweater, came across, and introduced himself.

'Craig Hooper. Sort of work in finance. They've unchained me from my desk for a while.' Meanwhile, Captain Pearce went with Chief Steward Peter Haynes, to be introduced to the other passengers.

'Welcome aboard, pleased to meet you, I said. 'My wife Jane.' Jane stepped forward and shook hands.

'It'll be good to get away from grey winter skies for a while Mr Hooper,' she said.

'Craig, do call me Craig. You'll be familiar with ships. This is my first big ship experience.

'I'm not unacquainted with ships. Both my father and husband are seafarers.' Laughter came from across the room. I felt, that it was more like Peter was working his magic than Captain Pearce.

'Believe it or not I'm as you say a duplicate Captain,' I joined in with. My responsibilities are more for the running of the ship.'

'And the passengers, perhaps?' he replied.

'Wouldn't exactly put if like that,' I said, 'but here to be of assistance – as we all will be Mr – I mean, Craig.' Already, at this point I was glad that Jane was with me to soften, you might say, my bluff approach to matters and this cargo type, namely passengers, who would ask questions and require plenty of social conviviality. On previous occasions, where on board receptions were given on board ship for civic dignitaries and company office staff, I had been advised that I should work the room. I'd never successfully acquired that skill of extrovert bonhomie, so suggested.

'My husband, is more accustomed to being aboard a work horse tanker or bulk carrier than this more sophisticated type of ship,' said Jane.

'Now, you see, for me, that I find, very interesting,' replied, Craig Hooper.

'Variety is the spice of life, as they say,' I quickly came in with. 'It's company policy to have us move around varied ship types within the fleet. I've no particular preference,' which was untrue,

'And anyhow Jane, would rather be aboard a cargo passenger than oil tanker?'

'Come on Mike, I'm happy to swap drizzly old England for sunny climes. Consider myself lucky to have the opportunity of a trip.

'You don't normally accompany Mike then?' I came in here.

'Blue Circle line offer Captain's an opportunity to take their spouse, every so often. Actually, Captain Pearce has allowed Jane to accompany me, instead of his wife, which we really appreciate. May I ask are you holidaying Craig?'

'Yes and no. Really great to get away from the office, but we, I mean Basset and Jones, my employers, have cargo aboard and I'm accompanying it. Can't really say more than that.'

'Quite, obviously that's a business confidentiality. You're able to mix business with pleasure, which is great. We don't have the range of bars and restaurants like aboard a passenger liner. Recreation facilities are a swimming pool, deck golf and of course warm tropical weather, once we get away from this.' I raised my hand toward a window, where droplets of rain, now and then, joined forces and ran down the glass.

'I intend to catch up on books I've meant to read over the years,' said Jane.

'Yes, I've considered this an opportunity to plough through Gibbons Decline and fall of the Roman Empire,' said Craig Hooper.

'There, you two already have something in common,' I said.

'That we read?' said Jane.

'Well, yes.'

'My reading's a bit lighter. More Agatha Christie. Mystery thrillers, that type of thing.

'That's even better' I said you will have different topics to talk about, perhaps.' We arrived, in the orbit of the introductory round of passengers from Chief Steward to Captain Pearce.

'Craig.' He extended his hand toward where we were stood. It didn't surprise me that Peter was already on friendly first name terms with Mr Craig Hooper. An ability to be on good terms with everyone was a hallmark of Chief Steward Peter Haynes' personality, you could say. It was really, in my estimation, no accident that he was Chief Steward, aboard Albany Contessa, the company's flagship. Peter continued,

'I'd like to introduce you to Captain Pearce.' Whatever, the issues were about Dougie or more appropriately Captain Pearce and his memory loss, there was no doubt he cut a striking figure in uniform. Unlike myself, he retained a dazzling head of white hair, further bleached by tropical sun, chiselled mahogany face and figure bearing, that you might expect of a sergeant major, on parade. I could see that Jane was impressed with his physicality, for his age and that there might be comment later, about my carrying over much weight.

'Captain Pearce – may I introduce you to, Mr Craig Hooper, Chief Financial Officer for Basset and Jones, Henley on Thames.

'Ah Mr Hooper, I might be seeking your advice, whilst aboard, I'm shortly to retire. So, they tell me,' Captain Pearce stepped forward and shook Craig Hoopers hand, who gave a short bow, as if he was about to meet with royalty.

'So nice to meet with you Captain Pearce and to be aboard your ship. I'd be pleased to offer advice on retirement matters. If I can't answer any of your questions, my head office, I'm sure, will help out.'

'Splendid, but let's not spoil your time aboard with unnecessary financial talk. I expect you want to escape from the soot of city life. I believe your trip is part business though?'

'I have to meet with business partners in Lagos, yes Captain.'

'But that's later. Hope to see you with a sun tan, before then – and properly relaxed, yes?'

'Thank you, Captain Pearce,' he replied. I couldn't see what he had to thank Dougie for, but he was caught up in some aura of respect that embodied a meeting with a ship's captain. Myself and Jane were like a couple of understudies alongside the actual ship's master. He turned back after a few paces.

'You'll be joining me for the evening meal?' Asked Captain Pearce.

'Well thank you Captain.' A smile spread across Craig Hoopers, face, as if he'd won first place in a class competition. Captain Pearce, turned to Peter,

'Chief Steward, Mr Hooper can be excluded from the passenger table rota and have a permanent place on my table.' Only three passengers dined on the captain's, table, at a time. The privilege shared among the nine passengers on a rota basis.

'Of course, if that's acceptable to you Craig,' he said, turning back to speak. It was a combination of this table offer and Captain Pearce's call by first name, that would have clinched a smile coverage, to both of Craig Hooper's cheeks.

'Perfectly acceptable Captain Pearce, sir. Thank you,' he replied.

Captain Pearce, glanced at the clock, set above the bar.

'Chief Steward. Have the steward sound the dinner gong will you. Peter walked over to the bar himself and removed the highly polished gong, from its stand. Held it out, in his left hand and at first gently tapped with the hammer, to produce a muffled, pitched sound, which increased, as conversational sounds lessened. The resonance of the gong stopped by his hand being placed across the gongs surface.

'Captain Pearce. Ladies and gentlemen passengers, officers – your evening meal is now ready to be served in the Dining Saloon. Thank you.'

Chapter 6

Steam Vessel Albany Contessa's Dining Saloon, was set in the ships after structure. Both, Captain Pearce's and adjacent table were next to windows which overlooked the after deck and number five hold. Two identical tables, which seated nine.

A long trestle-like table faced the near bulkhead, on entry for lower ranks. Already familiar with this dining saloon layout from when I worked as relief First Mate, around the coast aboard Contessa. Not dissimilar to other company ships saloons, save that it was more spacious, to accommodate both more officer crew, and passengers. Contessa carried four refrigeration officers, in addition to six engineer officers and could accommodate twelve passengers. Décor was also at a higher level, with polished mahogany and pine bulkheads. A shield with the company's crest placed just beneath the deckhead, with back strut support. The shield between the two senior officers and passenger tables. Each table chair anchored to the floor with a red leather covered chain. Silver condiment sets, with the company's crest, together with place settings, adorned tables. Ten could be seated either side of the trestle table. Passengers generally sat at the two senior level tables, but it was not unknown for younger passengers to migrate and sit on the long trestle table, maybe to escape perceived stuffiness encountered at senior level tables.

Captain Pearce and passengers walked ahead of Jane and me. So much for our introduction to the passengers. Captain Pearce for all the talk of memory loss was conversant with the need to get ahead. This need made apparent when the outer deck door opened, into the corridor, and a boiler-suited Bill Cooper entered.

'Just caught you. Mike, the pilot's aboard and we're to leave in forty minutes time.'

'You want me to tell Captain Pearce, Bill?'

'Yep. Not exactly equipped to go into the Dining Saloon,' hand, pointed toward his boiler suit.

'It wouldn't bother me,' said Jane. That probably wouldn't be the case for Captain Pearce, though.

'I'd like some time to check the deck area, while we proceed through the dock, if that's okay,' he said. 'That's before taking over the watch.'

'Okay Bill,' I said. 'I'll tell the old man.' Second Mate Bob Mitchel was just leaving the Dining Saloon and Bill intercepted him. Immediacy of departure was apparent when we entered the saloon and an approach view, of the stern tug's white housing, could be seen through the window. Captain Pearce was seated and talking to a passenger, assigned to his table. The stern tug's arrival, made no secret of, our near, departure. I followed Jane into the dining saloon. Captain Pearce was explaining some ship manoeuvre, I presumed, to the seated passengers, with a salt and pepper pot and a knife laid in between.

'Some news Captain Pearce, sorry to interrupt, Mr Cooper's informed me that the pilot's aboard and has proposed to leave in forty minutes time.' My first words before I sat opposite to Captain Pearce. He, nodded, in acknowledgement, and addressed the passengers having assessed the situation.

'You will have to excuse our impertinence, myself, Chief Rogers and Captain Peters, will need to be served straight away, and thank you Captain Peters.' Heads of departments were on the captain's table, which included Chief Engineer Chris Rogers.

That's perfectly alright, we understand, don't we Helen,' said Daniel Musgrove. The two passengers, included with Craig Hooper and allowed first attendance at the captain's table.

'Of course,' came from Craig Hooper. There was a pause,

before Helen said

'Is that right? You two met first met aboard a ship.'

'Whose been talking about us?' I asked, knowing full well it must have been Peter Haynes, Chief Steward, sat at table. The question was directed toward Jane.

'Yes, my father replaced a Captain Smith, aboard Albany Princess and I decided to work my passage.'

'First time I've heard of a young woman working her passage. Yes, I'll have the soup,' Captain Pearce said, in reply to the saloon steward, who held a menu in front of him.

'How romantic. Don't you think Daniel?' Daniel Musgrove, was Nigerian and Helen, I later learnt was from Kensington, London.

'Certainly is. And you became like girlfriend and boyfriend on board?' he asked.

'No, that was later. Mike was visiting Rosario as Second Mate aboard Ocean Melody.'

'How thrilling,' replied Helen.

'Not sure everyone wants to hear about our early lives,' I said dismissively. I didn't want mine and Jane's lives to become a main topic at table, and as it were, steal Captain Pearce's thunder. I interposed with,

'Captain Pearce, tells me you're returning home to Nigeria. You must both be looking forward to that?'

'Yes, we are,' said Helen. Captain Pearce, meanwhile was in conversation with Craig Hooper. Chief Engineer Chris Rogers, maintained what might be described as, a patient smile, while at table.

'I'll go straight for the Chicken Kedgeree,' said Peter. The steward, worked his way around the table, and marked each order on a pad. Conversational flow ceased while orders were being taken. 'Really looking forward to taking advantage of the swimming pool,' said Helen, once the steward had departed to the galley.

'Not so keen on deck golf,' though.

'I've brought a case full of books I've always meant to read,' said Jane.

'Very sensible,' Captain Pearce remarked.

'Perhaps we can swap? Do you read mystery thrillers?' He asked.

'Anything really, said Jane. Ended up reading a Whitacker's Almanac, seem to remember, when I'd got through Albany Princess's library.

'Then, you'll be good at Pub quizzes, with all that knowledge,' said the captain.

'Make sure that Jane's on my team Chief Steward, when you next organize a match.'

'Certainly Captain Pearce,' said Peter.

'Not sure how much knowledge stuck, though,' said Jane.'

'Ah, fresh blood, new knowledge. No, you'll be an advantage to either team, I'm sure,' he replied. As the meal progressed toward dessert Captain Pearce announced,

'We'll have to leave you in the capable hands of our Chief Steward.' That was never going to be a problem. I found out later that Chief Rogers and Captain Pearce were not averse to getting into a sparring match, over some difference of opinion. Not necessarily about shipboard matters. It could be at a political level, with regard to some government policy one or other did not favour. Peter Haynes, Chief steward, was well practised in passenger protocol. Captain Pearce, turned to the saloon steward, when he arrived with the sweet course.

'We'll forgo coffee.' Not a royal affirmation, but recognition that both the captain, myself and Chief Engineer would shortly leave. I gently squeezed Jane's arm to attract attention.

'I'm alright Mike. Meet up later,' she said. I joined Captain Pearce and Chief Engineer Rogers in getting up from my chair, whilst I heard Peter describe finer details of a new house, which included a swimming pool, to Jane and the three passengers.

On bridge arrival, a wheelman was in position. Bill Cooper could be seen, further forward, at the ship's bow leant over the starboard fo'c'sl'e, chatting to the tug's skipper. When we entered the wheel house, from the chart room, the pilot turned toward Captain Pearce and said,

'Good evening, Captain, you need to vacate the berth straightaway.'

'That's why we're here pilot.' The Third Mate walked in from the starboard bridge.

'Tell the Second Mate, he can let go lines.'

'Yes sir,' replied the Third, who got on to the blower to the Second, at the ship's stern.

First Mate Bill Cooper received a megaphone blast of,

'You can let go, Mr Cooper,' who returned receipt of instruction from the fo'c'sl'e, with a wave. Captain Pearce seemed to have a firm control of the situation, at this point. A well-practised departure ensued, in the hands of the pilot.

Chapter 7

I stayed on the bridge's watch keeping duty, up to when the pilot left to board the pilot cutter. It was seven fifteen. The senior apprentice was on the wheel and we were into the Irish Sea. Traffic approach from the south was constant and necessitated course alterations. Once the pilot disembarked, I decided to be officer, of the watch, to await, Bill Cooper, who was attending to a final check on deck. It was 1915. The Third Mate cross referenced with me, whilst the pilot was aboard, although not in a way that suggested insubordination toward Captain Pearce.

A choppy sea, was not sufficient to disrupt the ship into more than a gentle yawing motion, up and down. Passengers unaccustomed to motion aboard a ship would probably, not find it unpleasant. Once the pilot disembarked, via the pilot cutter, Captain Pearce, satisfied that, his ship, was on course and, with favourable weather conditions, departed with the words,

'Need to don my passenger friendly cap again.'

I chatted with Steven Prior, Third Mate, who'd recently served aboard one of the company's oil tankers. Unlike myself, he was glad to be aboard a ship which gave shore leave, opportunity, in foreign ports. Age difference, no doubt did play a role in our varied viewpoint. I agreed with his observation. At his age I would've have been keen to have time in foreign ports. The senior apprentice handed the wheel over to an AB earlier and was given the job to plot course positions, every fifteen minutes, together with the Third. At 1930, or thereabouts I said,

'You can go below for a break Third Mate; I'll keep watch and hand over to Mr Cooper. You're back on at 2000,' I said. It being, a First Mate's watch of 1600 to 2000. A Third Mate's watch keeping at sea, was 0800 to 1200, in the morning and

2000 to midnight, evening watch.

'I'll hand over,' I continued. The Third, wasted no time to vacate via the port bridge door, with the words,

'Thanks Captain Peters.'

Although, it would have been perfectly feasible, to be in a more observational role and not take control of the bridge away from the Third, I felt my role, in the circumstances, required a more hands on approach. I was wanting to meet up with First Mate Bill Cooper again on a more one to one basis; though, not a likely event, at this moment. Position checks were needed. every fifteen minutes and there was plenty of north bound traffic to watch out for. Course alterations, led to a need for complementary adjustment of ship's heading, to enable a return to the course line plotted on the chart Engine room was on Stand By.

Bill Cooper entered the Chart Room at about 1940 and from the wheelhouse I heard the words,

'Free, free, escaped at last.' He called out to no one in particular. Senior apprentice, Rick Taylor was glued to the wheelhouse radar screen, but awaiting instructions from the Mate. Bill's virtual soliloquy, resonated with my sentiment, after dealings with stevedore managers. That, underlying sense, that pandemonium could easily break out over any criticism of loading conditions, and lead to unseen delay. As First Mate, having to not exactly intervene, more give encouragement for load/discharge to continue, whilst not unduly, upsetting – management, foreman, crane driver or stevedore! Not only was it a relief to leave the hassle behind, but also to reach open waters where a pilot was no longer required.

'Midships.' I called out to the wheelman. Another alteration was about to throw Albany Contessa off course, momentarily. The ship ahead, now showed its port navigation light after veering to starboard in response to my alteration. I took a look at the giro and said to the wheelman.

'Steady on one nine five.'

'Steady on one nine five, it is then,' came back the reply and he proceeded to give port rudder to counteract further bow swing.

'Busy out here then,' said Bill when he entered the wheelhouse.

'To be expected,' I said. 'At least visibilities good.'

'Right.' It wasn't a time for pleasantries. I pointed out lights from three ships. Light visible from the bridge. These were not likely to interfere with Albany Contessa's passage. Meanwhile, Bill talked with the senior apprentice before sending him below. The ship that I altered course for across on our port side. When in the chart room, away from the wheelman's ears, Bill asked.

'Everything go okay with Dougie?' I didn't want to be seen to condone first name familiarity and said,

'Captain Pearce allowed the pilot free rein. There wasn't any situation which wasn't straightforward.

'Might be different at Lagos.'

'We'll meet that when and, if it arises. I've authority from head office to step in should the need require it.'

'That sounds alright, on dry land. Ship's Captain is master of all he surveys etc...Anyway, it stressed poor old Tim out, that's for sure.'

'Do you think so?'

'Most likely.'

"Light thirty degrees on port bow,' the voice of the Lookout, which sounded, in the wheelhouse made us both leave for the bridge. It was most likely the mast head light of an approaching ship.

'We're on 195 but need to get back to 185. If this one hadn't arrived, I'd have gone for 165, to address the alteration,' I said and trained binoculars on the light just as a port navigation light appeared above the horizon, as did Bill.

'That's looking better. Traffic's clearing generally,' I said.

'Got the picture. Course is 195. We're on Stand By and need to get back on course with adjustment. I'll take that Captain Peters.'

'Right then it's all yours,' I said.

'You've a wife below who'll be wondering where her husband's got to.'

'That might not be her view. Anyway, Bill I'll have a look at the cargo manifest, tomorrow, after breakfast.

'Sure. That's fine by me.'

Chapter 8

I returned to my cabin. Jane wasn't there, but on the table, in the day room was a note, which read – "Mike – in Smoke Room, if you want to find me" – Love Jane x. I did want to find her and made my way there. Although, the evening meal was over, an aroma of smells, which included that of roast meat lingered in the corridor from the adjacent dining saloon on my approach. A boiler suited engineer, said 'good evening, sir,' on passing. The eyes of two apprentices, sort of swivelled in my direction, from inside a cabin, with its door open, as I walked past. The senior apprentice, having, no doubt appraised them of my arrival, aboard from when he was on the bridge. There were four deck apprentices aboard Albany Contessa, who came under First Mate's Bill Coopers's area of responsibility. I heard Jane's voice as I approached the Smoke room.

'Did you really? Jane was sat across from, a black/ grey haired, vivacious older woman. She turned and smiled at me, as I entered. Two engineer officers were playing darts at the far end whilst the bar steward vigorously polished wine glasses, before he stretched up and hooked them back to their position, above the bar. Doctor Robert Sinclair and his wife Lucy, were sat at a table, in the far corner.

'My husband returns,' she said, as I reached out to shake the older woman's hand.

'Jackie Braithwaite,' she said, 'we haven't met.'

'Very pleased to meet you, Jackie. I sat down next to Jane.

'A regular Blue Circle passenger, I'm told,' and gave a sort of, wide eyed look of appreciation.

'That's right and Jane tells me you met aboard ship. Perhaps I'll have some luck like that. No, not really, I couldn't cope with long absences. I think you probably need to be from a seafaring background, don't you?'

'It probably helps,' I said

'You've sailed, with Captain Pearce aboard the Contessa before I understand?'

'Oh yes, but this will my first visit to Lagos. I'm sort of attached to the ship and quite happy to go where ever she goes. There was a pause in the conversation, before she continued.

'I don't want to appear rude, but I have had rather a long day. I hope you don't mind if I leave you.' Jane replied.

'No, we quite understand. We're the same. It's been a hectic day, for us two travelling to the ship, hasn't it Mike?' I nodded in agreement and made to rise from my chair, as Jackie Braithwaite, got up from hers.

'No, do stay where you are, please. I'm just going to ask Max if he'll make me a cocoa.' Max being the passenger steward behind the bar. The two engineer officers who were previously playing darts were now sat talking with Doctor Sinclair and his wife. Jackie, kind of waved to wish them a good night. I didn't consider it necessary to introduce myself and anyway, I'm sure Jane would have made them aware of who I was. We decided to follow Jackie's lead and returned to our cabin. Jane opening the door with a key.

'We're at sea now,' I said.

'Maybe, but it's not just a ship's crew. We don't really know the passengers, do we?'

'True,' I said. Are you suspicious of anyone?'

'No, but I'm not sure I would totally trust all of them on a first meeting. And this is what it is.

'You've met, I mean talked to all of them then?' Jane, went to fill the kettle which was on an evening tray left by the steward and called back from the bathroom. There was a lurch and we both reached out and took hold of whatever part of the cabin was nearest. Jane grabbed the bathroom door handle and I, the back of the settee nearby.

Hit a bit of heavy sea by the feel of it. Not that unexpected,' I said. 'You've talked to them all then?'

'Yes. Pretty much. I'm having a cocoa like Jackie.'

'I'll join you, then.' While waiting for the kettle to boil, Jane started running through the passenger list, with her take on them, so to speak.

'Jackie's retired but apparently still tutors students.'

'Right. What about the couple with the engineers?' I asked.

'Robert and Lucy. He's a doctor. She's, his partner. Not sure what she does work wise, but they're aboard for the cargo passenger liner experience.'

Did you get to chat with the others?' I asked.

'Oh yes, well save for John Palmerston-Smyth. He wasn't happy, I heard him say to Peter, that he was given a single passenger cabin. Apparently, Blue Circle Line head office stipulated he could have a double. Peter sorted it out. He's very good at smoothing over the waters, isn't he?'

'There are spare cabins. We're not at full passenger capacity. Oh yes, Peter knows the art of diplomacy, in these matters. Not sure I'd have that sort of patience.'

'It's probably just as well you've got me with you to temper any impatience that might surface, then, don't you think Mike?

'If you say so.'

'I do! Now, Daniel Musgrove and Helen Taylor. They're a mysterious couple. I mean they appear as partners, but it might be more business than a personal relationship.' Jane continued a run through of the passengers.

'Is she Nigerian, I mean, by birth ...?

'I didn't find out that much, but she talked fondly about growing up there and it does appear that it's a return visit to their homeland. Stewart Hopkins and Paul Jenkins, I feel that they might be on a sort of fact-finding mission. I heard them talk about the future viability of refrigerated cargo liners.

'That's interesting. Past experience of passengers aboard cargo liners is that several can be relatives of the owners or employed by the company, in some capacity.'

'You don't recognize them from anywhere, then Mike?'

'No, can't recall ever meeting those two. Do appreciate your being on board, you know.'

'To smooth over your possible lack of relationship skills toward passengers? Is that what you mean Captain Peters?'

'You're pretty good at sleuthing, as well, it seems.' Jane walked across with a tray which contained two Blue Circle Line crested mugs of cocoa and a plate of biscuits. She placed the tray on the table next to the settee.

'Isn't it just great to be together. I mean the two of us,' she said after sitting down, next to me.

'Don't you miss Carol and Dinah?'

'Of, course I do, but they'll have a whale of a time, with father and mother and then Mike, normally I don't get to see you for months on end. I'm in no way complaining.'

'It is all about compromise, I suppose,' I said.

'How very philosophical of you. Are you compromising your role of newly appointed Staff Captain by having your wife aboard then?' Jane smiled, with that look of be careful what you say, as she handed me a mug of cocoa, and held out the plate of biscuits.

'You know I don't think that. Compromise is not the right word. More a golden opportunity for us to be together,' quickly rescuing the situation, from any idea that Jane interfered with my role aboard ship. It could be that a husband might not want his wife in close proximity to his place of work or vice-versa. Jane, understood those demands placed on a professional seafarer, having grown up with a seafaring father. Seafaring is a way of life, which makes demands beyond that of a nine to five workplace, where home life has a regularity.

'What's got into you Mike? You're Captain aboard the company's flag ship.'

'Staff Captain, I need to remind you. Not actual Captain.'

'As good as,' I hadn't told Jane, about the situation with Captain Pearce, although, perhaps intuitively, she understood, as women can, that my role was more than that of shadowing Captain Pearce.

Chapter 9

'You, can have a ten-minute break, before you go off watch, but need you back up here to hot wash the windows.' I heard Bill, give these instructions, as I entered the chart room, early morning. Previously, the apprentice would have been on look-out duty. A spread of wheelhouse window was encrusted with brine, that had dried, now that the sun was up. Hot washing, was not as sophisticated as that of a car wash and required the fill of buckets of hot water and a clamber on the Monkey Island above, before water was flung on the windows. Several buckets of hot water were needed to completely clear brine from the wheelhouse windows.

It was pre-breakfast and I wanted to meet up with Bill to find out more about the cargo aboard and anything else that might be of interest. My appointment was short notice. Sister ship, Albany Viscountess, was the only other vessel with a Staff Captain, and Viscountess was in South America. Appointment to Staff Captain was a definite step up the ladder, but I needed to reacquaint myself with the finer points of being aboard a refrigerated cargo passenger liner, rather than more practical and specific demands of my previous ship, that of an oil tanker. Albany Contessa was on automatic pilot and we were the only two in the wheelhouse. Bill looked up from noting the course on the giro repeater, when I walked into the wheelhouse from the chart room.

'Good to see you, I'd hoped we'd get a chance to talk,' he said.

'Yes,' I said. 'Are you expecting Captain Pearce?' A stiff formality, aboard Contessa seemed to have replaced, a familiar "old man," moniker, where Captain's, are called this, outside their hearing, regardless of age. Captain Pearce did, in this instance, meet that requirement.

'He sometimes visits during the eight to twelve to take a sun sight, but not that frequently. I've to get, sand paper, brushes, varnish and scrapers from the Bosun. Captain Pearce, plans to rub down and re-varnish the mahogany, bridge and boat deck rails outward bound.

'Won't he be with the passengers? I mean, entertaining them?'

'Yes. But well, there's a Staff Captain – and his wife, I've noticed.' Bill smiled, in my direction.

'Expect, he feels he can relax and do a bit of housework, so to speak.' Bill turned to answer a question from an apprentice, who held a bucket of steaming water.

'Two lots should do it, yes.' He'd asked, if two lots of hot buckets of water, would be sufficient to clear the brine? I continued.

'I see. Was that Tim's role then? I mean entertaining the passengers?'

'Pretty much. He had a movie projector and brought along a few films to show passengers and crew. Gave lectures about ports and countries he'd visited.'

'They won't be getting that level of entertainment from me,' I said.

'Don't worry yourself, Captain Peters, there's deck golf and then you have Jane with you. Tim, could be a bit too friendly toward the drink. Don't get me wrong. He had it under control, whatever you might hear from Dougie.'

'The old man,' I referred to the captain in this way, 'does seem to believe it was drink, which did for his liver.'

'I'm not sure. There have been stressful situations on the bridge. On occasion Tim said he questioned one or two of Dougie's instructions, when he went against the pilot's decision.'

'In Lagos?'

'No, it was Liverpool. And you know how reliable the pilots are?

'It's in the remit of a Captain to overrule a pilot's instructions, when he's in disagreement, as you know, save when going through Panama when responsibility is totally given over to the Canal authorities.'

'Yes, but with memory lapse, Captain Pearce can lose the plot. It used to be momentary lapses, but last trip there were two bridge incidents where Tim had to step in and takeover, to support the pilot.'

'I witnessed no problem leaving port this time.'

'It's entering usually, but heigh-ho, only two more port visits to go, and Dougie will be anchored ashore. I just want to make sure that you're aware of when and where Captain Pearce might lose the plot. It also, makes it high on the agenda, for you Captain Peters and your wife, to be more involved with the passengers, if you don't mind me saying so, "sir." It was probably best that Bill addressed me formally in this way at the time. As the saying goes the buck stopped with me.

Bill, picked the binoculars from their holster, to take a closer look at a freighter. Evidently, there'd been an understanding between Bill and previous Staff Captain, Tim Burroughs, on how to handle, decline in Captain Pearce's short-term memory.

'Thought he might do that.' Although, well on Contessa's starboard bow ahead, and able to clear easily, a freighter decided to veer to starboard, which led to a display plume of white at its bow. Bill, replaced the binoculars and responded by giving five degrees of starboard wheel and a blast on the ship's whistle. Rule of the Road recognition, whereby vessels sound a blast when visible to an approaching ship and altering to starboard or two blasts when the course is altered to port. Our conversation ended, while Bill steadied the ship well to starboard of the freighter

We were heading south and meeting up with north bound traffic, which was heading back to the UK. After the freighter settled across on the port side our chat continued. I didn't want to make an issue of the situation with regard to Captain Pearce, after all this was his last trip before retirement, but hoped I could handle it, with carefully with consideration. I was a visitor to the bridge and not officer of the watch.

'Bill.'

'Yes, Captain Peters.' I was accustomed to being addressed as Chief or Mr Mate and it almost caught me off guard when addressed as Captain. Bill Cooper, was returning Albany Contessa to her previous course line. The Third Mate could be heard in the chart room. It was near to eight.

'Like to know about the cargo situation, after breakfast.'

'Interesting.' He replied – 'what there is of it. I intend to check it out. See if all's well below decks. There's been quite a bit of rocking and rolling through the night.'

'Yes, managed to do for some of the passengers,' I said. I'd noted a few absences at yesterday's midday and evening meal.' Bill scanned the forward horizon with binoculars, as he spoke. He was about to hand over the watch to Steve Prior, Third Mate.

'I'll be in my cabin, Bill.'

'Right, be there,' he said, and turned to the Third, as he walked into the wheelhouse from the chart room and had begun to point out ships in view. I walked to the port bridge and made a grab for the companionway rail, as the ship recovered from a deep bow dive, into oncoming waves. I noticed a spread of damp across part of the boat deck, from night rain once down the stairway. Both lifeboats were uncovered, with the ship out of port. I made for an outer accommodation door and followed the corridor which led to my cabin door.

'Is that you Mike?' Jane called from the bedroom, as I opened and shut the door.

'Who were you expecting?' I asked.

'Don't be silly. We can breakfast together.' Jane emerged from the bedroom dressed in a print tee shirt matched and navy skirt.

'The ship's motion hardly affected you, as I remember, aboard Albany Princess.'

'But it did you,' she smiled, in reply.

'You remember that far back?' I sat on a day bed, situated under the front facing window, whilst Jane stood before a wall mirror, to judge whether the top and skirt met with approval. It did to me, but my opinion, probably incidental, at that point, in the wider scheme of things.

Yes, you were one of the early ones to leave the dining saloon, as I remember when, that kind of corkscrew motion got going

'And you stayed almost as long as Tom.'

'So, you do remember?'

'Not something that I can easily forget. Those early days at sea, seem as vivid, as yesterday.'

'That's good Mike. Isn't it? Having decided that her breakfast attire met with approval Jane called across,

'You need a shave. We're aboard the company's flagship. Not some oil tanker. You can't appear in the Dining Saloon, like that.'

'A shave was on the agenda.' For which I received a brief kiss on the cheek.

'Yes definitely. Aren't you glad, I'm here to give advice on decorum and appearance, in your new role?'

'I am,' I said, and meant it.

Chapter 10

Albany Contessa was no longer ploughing through Atlantic rollers, and Chief Engineer Chris Rogers was just ahead of us when we entered the Dining saloon.

'That window needs closing.' He pointed toward a top window on one side of the saloon. There were windows across the back bulkhead (wall), similar to the front housing on Contessa.

'Yes Chief,' said the saloon steward who walked across from where he stood to shut the window. On noticing us behind, he said,

'The air con's running. I've, the Sixth Engineer tasked to tell everyone.'

'It certainly feels cooler in here already,' said Jane. Chief Rogers remark, I felt, about the Sixth Engineers role was for my benefit. Earlier, peremptory manner, toward the steward melted away, and produced, a smile, on realization that Jane was with me. A few were sat on the long officer's table. Bill Cooper's table, next to Captain Pearce's was fully occupied. The captain's table, which we joined, seated three passengers; Craig Hooper, Daniel Musgrove and Helen Taylor. I'd met Craig at first reception, but not the other two properly who smiled at Jane, evidently, the three of them were well acquainted.

'Hi, I've got my other half with me,' she said. It was a way of breaking the ice.

'No, stay where you are,' I said. Daniel Musgrove was in the midst of standing up, to shake hands. I decided to sit in a vacant chair next to his, whilst Jane entered immediately into conversation with Helen, before she sat down next to her. I shook hands with Daniel Musgrove, which seemed overly formal. I noticed that Chris Rogers was talking to Craig, which meant that he was not excluded. The other passengers,

Stewart Hopkinson and Paul Jenner, Doctor and Mrs Lucy Sinclair, all of whom I met to talk with after breakfast, were on the adjacent senior officer table. Jacqueline Braithwaite, sat next to the Third Engineer, on the all-other officer ranks table, together with three of the apprentices. She didn't hesitate to give Jane a wave. Later, entrance of John Palmerston Smyth, subdued the atmosphere, for me, at any rate.

'We've captured some better weather for you. Good morning, everyone,' were Captain Pearce's first words as he entered the dining saloon. The steward who was about to take a breakfast order from an apprentice, broke away to be by Captain Pearce's chair on his arrival. Captain Pearce, didn't look at the menu.

'I'll start with a tomato juice, steward,' he said, before announcing,

'It's so much better outside than yesterday. We've put distance in from British weather, I'm pleased to say.' It seemed a strange expression, "better outside," as if we were in a country house and not aboard a ship. But then Captain Pearce, might well be acquainted with a country estate, being married to the owner's cousin, and anyway, I was out of touch with life, aboard a cargo passenger liner. Not just any cargo passenger, the flagship, no less! No mention was made of absences in the dining saloon due to the motion of the ship in the past twenty-four hours.

'Captain Pearce, sat down and picked the serviette from the table, determinedly flicked it open and placed it on his lap before asking,

'Deck golf, does deck golf appeal to you Craig?'

'Yes, Captain. I seem to have got my sea legs.

'Will you be playing Captain?'

'I'll most probably bring on a substitute.' I was made aware of whom that would be, when he looked toward me and Jane. Conversation, died on the table when Captain Pearce arrived.

Out of respect for his being head of table, more than any other reason.

'Do carry on everyone,' he said, when the steward arrived with the tomato juice.

'I'll have some Worcester sauce steward. The steward produced a bottle from his other hand and placed it on the table.

'Good lad, you know my preference for Worcester sauce. Gives it that extra bite, I find.'

'Everyone had a good night's sleep, I hope?' The question was addressed to the passengers and Daniel Musgrove replied.

'Certainly, did Captain. Just knowing that, no one can telephone, does it for me.'

'Sparks, regularly updates me with Head Office missives, but that's really it, communications wise. I've ship to shore radio, but no more of that for a while. Yes, it's good to escape that continuous intrusion of shore life.'

'I agree,' said Helen, who partnered Daniel Musgrove. Jane, later discovered that she was, his secretary, but now in the role of partner. Unlike Doctor and Mrs Lucy Sinclair they were not seasoned cargo liner passengers. Twelve days at sea might prove a long time away from shore life, and a test for their relationship, going forward. The three passengers and Chief Engineer Chris Rogers finished breakfast ahead of Captain Pearce, Jane and myself. Captain Pearce, did though manage to get all three passengers in agreement to meet on the boat deck for a game of deck golf at eleven, hosted by myself and Jane. There was still time enough to check out the cargo with Bill between times and I left Jane, sat with Jackie in the Dining Saloon with Captain Pearce. Chief Steward Peter Haynes was having coffee with several passengers in the Passengers lounge. Captain Pearce stipulated, that tropical whites, would be dress of the day, starting from today.

By the time Bill knocked on our cabin door, I was in a white boiler suit over white tropical uniform. My itinerary for the morning included a game of deck golf with the passengers, as mentioned, but that was not until eleven, which left just over an hour to inspect the ship's cargo, which I knew from Bill to be in four of the five normally refrigerated holds.

'I've a copy of the cargo manifest,' said Bill. 'Not that complicated, but valuable.'

'How is that?' I asked.

'Well apart from very everyday crates of machinery parts and medical equipment, mainly cased or crated there are ten thousand cases of wire caged palleted gold ingots. Ten ingots per case. They're distributed in number one, three, four and five holds. One thousand cases in one and three. Four thousand in four and five. Marked up as agricultural machine parts, but with matched codes across the boxes, not to mistake gold for genuine machine parts. All pallets wire caged, ready for discharge when we arrive in Lagos.

'Have they emptied the vaults of the bank of England?' I asked.

'Looks like that.'

'I guess. Refrigeration's not on, is it?

'It's at a temperature rated as ambient to avoid condensation. Although, Number Two holds – being tested, at maximum refrigeration level, by the fridge engineers.'

'I'd like to take a look, starting at Number one.'

'You may need a duffle coat and hat.' Tim Burroughs had left two duffle coats and matching woolly hats in the double wardrobe. I removed one set.

'Need to pick mine up, on the way,' said Bill. I tried one duffle for size. It was a good fit.

I followed Bill, through the corridor and down to the next deck to his cabin.

Memories, flooded back, to when aboard one of the company's other refrigerated liners, as I went with Bill, down ladders, that eventually led to the third deck of cold chambers in number one hold. It could be a welcome relief to descend into the cold of the refrigerated chambers in tropical climates. At times, hatches would need to be closed, when refrigerated meat or produce was being loaded in port to maintain the cold. Bill carried a torch, but the chambers were lit.

That batch; Bill flashed his torch toward a spread of crates in the chamber, is probably worth one hundred million pounds. Each pallet with a recessed loading bar for a cargo hook to attach itself to.

'Quite a lengthy procedure loading or unloading each caged pallet, individually,' I said.

'Yes, but only specifically marked pallets will be so high value. They're not unaccompanied. Passenger Craig Hooper is a representative for the company which owns the ingots.'

'That might explain why Captain Pearce has Craig on his table.'

'What was that?' Bill missed my remark, he was inspecting lettering on a crate.

'Not important,' I said.

'The ship manifest, lists the crates, as agricultural machinery parts. Detailed listing has been made of each pallet's contents, as particular agricultural parts, to make it appear genuine.'

'What about Customs? I asked.

'They're in on it, I'd bet. A subterfuge to bypass the true nature of the cargo. These ingots, are worth many times what the ship is worth.' Bill flashed his torch across a four deep stack, shored into position with 3x3 timber and wire. A long-printed code of letters and numbers was followed by a dash and a number or in this case numbers. I could see twenty, twenty-two and twenty-five.

'Was this the first batch to be loaded?'

'You've got it,' said Bill.

'Numbers and lettering printed in yellow from one to

a thousand, in this hold. In three hold the same Mike, but with green lettering; and in four, one to four thousand in red lettering and five hold, one to four thousand in blue, respectively. There's genuine agricultural machinery parts and hospital equipment amongst the gold. I could see what looked like galvanized gate parts and fencing tied together at the far end of the chamber. Bill continued.

'Their sheer weight holds them in place as much as anything.' Cages of palleted boxes, were corralled by 3x3 wooden struts to hold crossed planking in place.

'Nothing to report here to Dougie about cargo movement,' said Bill.

'You'll want a shifty at the other three cargo holds?' questioned Bill.

'If nothing else it's good exercise, and will acclimatize me to layout below decks, once more. Let's have a look at each deck level in all three holds,' I replied. I wasn't sure that Bill had this in mind and might well have already sent chippy below decks to make certain all was well. In his position, as First Mate, I might have done the same. However, with ten thousand crates of gold aboard I wanted to see each batch for myself. A somewhat more valuable boxed cargo than whisky and brandy.

Chapter 11

Although familiar with carrying ore and steel plate, gold ingots, was certainly a step up and I was surprised that such a valuable cargo, was allowed aboard. That the gold ingots were in cold chamber compartments, with printed description as agricultural parts created deception, and secrecy was kept about the true nature of the contents. I returned to my cabin, determined to get more information from Captain Pearce.

'Hurry up Mike.' I was greeted by Jane, in white shorts and pink top, as I entered our cabin.

'It's a quarter to eleven. We need to get out on to the boat deck.'

'Okay, okay,' I said. 'I've only got to get this duffle coat and boiler suit off.' Now out of the cold chambers, I was more than over dressed, and went to the bedroom to remove duffle coat and boiler suit.

Chief Steward, Peter Haynes was stood by a port side lifeboat when we stepped out on to the boat deck. I heard laughter as he talked with passengers, keen to play deck golf. Doctor Robert and Mrs Lucy Sinclair, Craig Hooper and Jacqueline Braithwaite. I was familiar with the game and we paired up. Jane with Jackie; the Sinclair's stayed together and I paired with Craig. Peter refereed, with a score card. This deck game, involved negotiating numbered circles. A form of clock golf, but on a deck with wooden chucks. Stewart Hopkins and Paul Jensen stayed aloof from our group. They chatted and smoked near to one of the two lifeboats.

'Ladies first,' said Dr Sinclair, who I'd say was mid-forties and wore gold rimmed glasses. Looked the part, with white cap and matched shorts, socks and tennis shoes. His wife, was younger and was dressed in blue denim fashion overalls; blond hair tied away from her face, in a ponytail. I wanted to know more about Craig's role in the transport of this large consignment of gold ingots. That was, if he was prepared to talk about it. We were stood back after we'd reached number three in the deck golf course, ahead of the others, at this point.

'Understand, that you're not purely a passenger Craig. You don't mind me asking?'

'No, Captain Peters, not a problem.' He nevertheless, moved his eyes to see if anyone else was close, before reply.

'I'm not sure that Captain Pearce appreciates the implications.' He said that crates and cases are a regular cargo and present less problems than refrigerated product.'

'There is that. Would you like to, take a stab at number four?' I pointed to the white number four on the circle just forward of a lifeboat. Craig positioned the chuck on the third circle at his feet and with the hammer between his legs and hit the chuck within inches of number four. I followed up by neatly hitting it in to the circle.

'Best shot so far,' called out Peter, who noted our score down. We were underneath a lifeboat.

'I'm concerned about who knows about the cargo – I mean the contents of the boxes in the caged pallets,' he said.

'Only three people,' to my knowledge. That's Captain Pearce, myself and First Officer Bill Cooper. We're the only ones with sight of the manifest and true nature of the cargo.'

'That,' – Daniel Musgrove, asked if I was in finance. When, we first met in the passenger lounge. It just seemed a strange question. Like, out of the Blue, Captain Peters. The company has made clear that I would be registered as a regular passenger with no connection with the cargo.'

'That's how it is,' I said. 'I mean there's no way passengers backgrounds and occupations would be public knowledge. Could it be that he was making conversation?' Craig Hooper struck me, as exactly the type of person who might be seen as in banking or finance.

'It's you to go again, Craig.' I replied,

'It felt,' he said, 'that he was trying, to establish, who I was, more than making conversation.' Craig made another superlative strike, on the chuck, which took it within a foot of the next deck circle.

'Sure, you haven't played this before?' I asked.

'You're way ahead of the field Mike,' Called out Chief Steward Peter Haynes.

'Beginners, luck, Captain Peters,' said Craig. I didn't encourage first name terms from the passengers, but it was unlikely that Peter was going to "Captain," me unless the occasion demanded, for example, in front of the crew. Memories, flooded back from sea college where we studied for certificates of competency. One class training officer decided that because there were so many instructors or college personnel, who previously held the role of Captain, from sea-going days, and expected to be addressed as such, he included students, in his appreciation and used to address us as captain. "And, could you define, Captain, what Declination is? (Sic. Declination – "arc of a celestial meridian, a body is north or south of the celestial equator") for the benefit of the class?" Or as a term of greeting – "Good morning, Captain." This address given to any, number of students.

I walked across and tapped the chuck into number five, on the deck.

'Personally, I think, the idea of stowing a valuable cargo in refrigerated compartments, is probably a good idea, because it seems an unlikely place. A swap of slabs of butter for...

'I'd rather, no mention is made about cargo, Captain Peters,' interrupted Craig.

'As you wish. I understand,' I said. By way of changing the subject, I asked,

'Have you always been in finance Craig?' We were several numbers ahead of the others and could afford to wait awhile, to let them catch up.

'No, I started in retail as a Saturday boy and went full time after leaving sixth form. My manager, at the time, asked if I intended staying as a store assistant. It got me thinking and I replied to an advert for banking staff, in our local newspaper.

'And the rests history,' as the saying goes,' I said.

'Yes, that's right. Well not quite. I moved about the country in branch banking, before a move into the investment side of the business. This transhipment belongs to a Nigerian client. He has government influence.'

'Then things could be a little more formal at the other end?' I asked.

'Definitely. We, that's the company, have negotiated, with the government for a military presence to escort the ingots from your ship to the bank vaults.

'Doesn't that advertise the value of the cargo?'

'Yes, but the alternative is that an attempt would be made to ambush the truck convoy to the bank. This is less likely with an escort of jeeps with machine gun emplacements.

'Yet, your company allowed the ingots to be loaded on pallets, as if they were an unexceptional cargo?'

'It was a calculated risk. A freight list for agricultural export, was accessed. Each crate shows up as containing, machinery compatible with a previous export made to South America.'

'The client wouldn't be the Nigerian government by any chance?' I asked.

'I'm not at liberty to say,' said Craig, which led me to believe that it probably was.

'Well done, Jackie.' I heard Jane call out. They'd caught us up.

'You've nothing to worry about,' called out Peter, who'd moved across to stand beneath the funnel.

'No pair are anywhere near your scores Mike.' The course numbered eight, which did not make it exactly clock golf.

'We'd better continue,' I said.

We maintained our lead, on the score chart; Jane and Jackie were second; followed by Doctor and Mrs Lucy Sinclair. Jane said that I'd an unfair advantage with having played before, aboard another of the company's refrigerated cargo liners. In all honesty, it was Craig who put in a stellar performance, not me.

Chapter 12

It was ever going to be the case that Jane would pal up with Jacqueline Braithwaite. Jackie was retired from teaching, and Jane was taking advantage of long summer school holidays to accompany me on board. A background in teaching and with similar interests, including that of motherhood. There was no sense of rivalry between the two of them. Jane was better acquainted with the passengers than I was and together with Jackie became formidable in organizing activities for the passengers outward bound to Lagos. A twelve-day trip for Albany Contessa out of Liverpool, with an average speed of sixteen knots. It had been made clear, by head office, that I was expected to oversee ship management, in and out of port, but a major role was also that of making sure that passengers were making the most out of their stay aboard. Deck golf was but one activity.

On the fourth day, out of Liverpool and luxuriating in the warmth of near tropical temperatures, I noted, where passsengers were enjoying afternoon tea on the funnel deck, Craig and Daniel stayed and played cards, in the corner of the Passenger and Officer Lounge. Officers and apprentices would be playing darts. Apprentices were invited, on occasion, to play a game of draughts or chess by either Doctor Sinclair or wife Lucy.

I was in a process of adjustment, in that this was the first time I'd been aboard a company ship, and not in that role of watchkeeper. As First Mate there was not only the four to eight watch to keep, but also ship maintenance work, to manage, with instructions given to Bosun and carpenter for daily supervision of tasks. The carpenter given assistance, when needed, by crew members and apprentices. That's not counting overall management of cargo loading or discharge, in port. There was a sort of role reversal in that I found it was me who was in the role of Bosun when I met up with Captain Pearce.

True, to Bill Cooper's information earlier, Captain Pearce was busy sanding down a mahogany rail, on the after bridge, away from passengers. It might have been suggested that Captain Pearce, was no longer fully in his role. This, was work, a deck hand, or even apprentice might have undertaken. Yet, he was in earshot of the bridge and with sight, of both fore and after deck area.

'How are you liking day work, instead of watch keeping Captain Peters?' Back and forth sand paper block motion, on mahogany rail, ceased, while, he spoke. In the eyes of passengers and crew, he was Captain and I, maybe, seen as some sort of substitute. More passengers' entertainment officer, than real ship's Captain. A Staff Captain wouldn't necessarily, be a first trip Captain, as I was. His manner, though old-fashioned and formal, was not meant, to patronize.

'Not missing early morning watches, then?' The early evening four to eight watch of First Mate, allowed time for unwinding and planning for the following day.' He ran his hand along the rail to gauge how smooth it was. He continued.

'Yes, watch keeping gives a pattern to life that is unchanging. Get a bit removed from that life, as Captain. Out of the blue he asked?

Do you intend staying at sea?'

'For the foreseeable future,' I replied.

'We're in a declining manufacturing country,' he remarked. 'Advances in technology will mean shipping companies won't be needing large crews. Although, that won't be my concern. Martha's set her eyes on a cottage in Devon. Holidayed there in the past and it will be removed from shipboard life.'

'That's something to look forward to then, at the end of the trip.'

'Not known life, other than working aboard a ship since

71

aged sixteen.' He continued sanding. I felt like I was interrupting his pastime, with realization that Captain Pearce was going through a period of adjustment with his ship's Captain position, to be relinquished at the end of this trip, when back in the UK. Thoughts, were perhaps towards retirement, and acknowledgement that he might not find this easy. An uncomplicated last trip lay ahead. I was not of an age to be concerned about retirement, but as pension providers stress, it's never too early to start saving for retirement. I wanted to know more about Craig Hooper, who was in finance.

'Came as a surprise to learn that there's such a large consignment of gold aboard.'

'It mustn't get out Peters. Only the three of us must know about it. The First Mate did tell you this?'

'I asked to see the manifest.'

'Right. It's best not talked about.'

'A big responsibility for Craig Hooper, though, I guess?'

'Yes, I'm under instructions to keep an eye on him.'

'That, I take it, is why he has a permanent place on your table?'

'Yes, we've no reason to suspect that he's at risk personally. Not while aboard the ship. It's the transit from ship to bank in Lagos that is more of concern. I won't be disappointed to see this consignment away from the ship and into a bank vault.'

'Have you carried gold as a cargo before?' I asked.

'Not as cargo. Nothing more than jewellery and small amounts of gold sovereigns, but held in the safe, not in the chilled compartments. It's a sign of how desperate the company is to secure a cargo, outward bound, I'd say.'

Chapter 13

"Captain Peters." – A voice, called from behind a lifeboat, which I recognized as Joe Blackburn. He first greeted Jane and me when we boarded. Part, of an old paint splattered tarpaulin was laid on an almost white wooden deck. Jack, was red leading railings, between two lifeboats. Railings, that were newly scraped and wire brushed.

'Not like Melody, sir.' Joe referred to Ocean Melody, the ship we served aboard, when I met up with Jane, again in Rosario.

'No, two to three weeks in port, in those days. These fridge boats don't hang around.'

'Disappointed?' I asked.

'Some of the young ones will – that's for sure. But it's for the best, where I'm concerned. Pay off with more. Like you, Captain Peters, have commitments, in the way of wife and kiddies. Do you have a family?'

'Two daughters. Being looked after by Mrs Peters parents.'

'That's nice. No offence sir, but hope they take after Mrs Peters, in looks.'

'They do. They're twins, and have more the temperament, of their maternal grandfather.'

'Ah, that'll be Captain Anderson.'

'Maybe, they'll follow their father and grandfather and become seafarers?'

'One of them might, you never know. Can see, more, opportunities for young women, to train and become ship's officers, than when you and me started out.'

'So true. But can see a time, with fewer crews, way things are going. Container ships and large tankers with low maintenance and quick turnarounds.'

'Just have to hope they want ships to be manned, in the future.' I decided to end our conversation. I could see Bill

Cooper or most likely the Bosun, getting tetchy about delaying Joe, in his ship's maintenance work.

'Won't hold you up Jack.' I continued my walk back to my cabin.

Jane was reading The Count of Monte Cristo. Time at sea gave opportunity to read those books you always wanted to read and never got around to. She looked up from reading.

'You do know, Mike there's a talk for passengers being given by Jackie about the Cornish Riviera in the Passengers Lounge this evening?' I did.

'Only the passengers?

'No off duty, officers can attend.'

'What about the crowd?'

'Jackie's very democratic. She's giving the same talk to the crew, tomorrow.

'You're expected to be there. Captain Pearce said could we be sure to attend, because he won't be able to make it.'

Rather than staying in the passengers' lounge when coffee was served, after the evening meal, while coffee was being served, I'd made visits to see Bill Cooper, on his four to eight. I noted, that Daniel Musgrove and Craig Hooper remained in the lounge playing cards after coffee was served. Gambling in the way of card playing was not encouraged for the crew, aboard ship. I was perhaps naïve to suppose it was an innocent game, without stakes being placed.

John Palmerston-Smyth, from Head Office, was very non-committal. He said that he was looking forward to better weather and made a point of sitting away from others, to listen to the world service from a speaker, in the corner of the lounge. It was hard work getting much out of him. I detected an accent in his voice, which I could not place, although he had this British sounding name. He kept apart from other passengers, but seemed keen to know about the ship from officers, who he got into conversation with, and their roles aboard. My

74

appreciation was that, as a Head Office executive, he might find being informed about life aboard, a change from office politics. I felt, at the same time, that he was self-contained, and not likely to suffer from loneliness. No point in offering him encouragement to take part in shipboard activities. An ideal passenger, in a way, to my way of reckoning.

The talk was entertaining and I was glad that Jacqueline Braithwaite could give a presentation, with slides. Not something I would have excelled at, aboard ship or anywhere else for that matter. Showing films, where the projector did the work, was more my territory.

Next morning, I breakfasted early, on orange juice, coffee and toast with marmalade, and before his watch ended decided to Join First Mate, Bill Cooper on the bridge. I recall, that we were on the port side, stood in a warm tropical breeze. A Liberian Tanker, probably under American ownership was falling behind. Contessa's, sleek hull, with turbine driven propeller gave speed of sixteen, to seventeen knots, against, the tanker's twelve to possibly fourteen. Paul Reade, Radio Officer, appeared from the wheelhouse through the wheel-house's sliding door.

'There's a Mayday call. A coaster's apparently in trouble, not far away. Out of control fire in galley. Can we make a rescue?'

'Is that it.' I pointed to the type written company headed note he held in his hand.

'From the coaster?'

'No, no, a Norwegian freighter's messaged that it's not got facilities to accommodate a coaster's ship's crew, and that our ship, Albany Contessa, a cargo passenger liner, is probably best equipped to make a rescue

'Let's have it Sparks – the message. He handed over the company headed page, which was biro ringed with the coaster's position of 10 degrees north and 26 degrees fifteen west.

'Shall I ring the engine room to say we're going on Standby?' Bill Cooper anticipated the situation. There was every possibility, in place, that we would be going to the rescue. I made that decision.

'Ring Stand By now, Chief. We'll update the Third Engineer.' There was every chance that the bridge would get a call from the engine room to ask what was happening. There was time for that later

'Go on standby and plot a course toward the coaster, as soon as possible. I'll notify Captain Pearce, meantime.' Bill went across to the telegraph and I heard it buzz as I left the bridge. My quickest approach to the Passenger Lounge was down a companionway to the boat deck, then into the accommodation. Once there I walked across the Lounge floor, where Captain Pearce was sat talking with Craig.

'Sorry to interrupt Captain Pearce,' I said. 'Sparks has picked up a Mayday call passed on from a Norwegian freighter. A coaster, with a galley fire out of control. We're best placed to attempt a rescue.' There was a momentary pause, before

'And?' he asked.

'The First Mate's – 'a sudden fall in tempo from the main engine, indicated Bill had slowed to half speed, in preparation to make a dramatic course alteration.

'Setting us on a course line, accordingly.'

'Carry on Captain Peter's. I'll be up shortly. Bit of excitement,' he remarked across to passengers and Chief Engineer Chris Rogers. I'd evidently made the right decision and if I hadn't Captain Pearce wasn't going to say. Craig made a remark, which seemed out of the ordinary, as I left to return to the bridge.

'Are you sure this is a genuine distress call?'

Back on the bridge, it was Bill who first sited black wisps of smoke on the horizon off the starboard bow.

'Got it,' he called out from within the wheelhouse. The ship was off automatic and back to having a wheelman. I could see the Bosun and two, day workers positioned on the fo'c'sl'e.

Captain Pearce arrived in the wheelhouse, shortly afterwards and Bill pointed out the smoke on the horizon.

'Have the Bosun prepare the gangway on the port side Mr Cooper.' They'll hopefully be in lifeboats, when we arrive? Bill immediately walked to the starboard bridge deck and called the Bosun on a loud hailer.

'Bosun have your men prepare the port gangway.'

A wave of acknowledgement, followed, with his departure from the fo'c'sl'e with both deck hands.

Chapter 14

The Norwegian freighter and other ships might have been closer to the distressed coaster, but Albany Contessa was better accommodated to take aboard a ship's crew, albeit not a large one. Full ahead had been resumed after Bill made a ninety degree plus course alteration to speed toward the coaster. Soon an oil marked dark blue hull with rust-streaked upper housing was visible on the horizon, a few degrees, on the starboard bow.

'Slow ahead.' Captain Pearce took command of the bridge. I trained binoculars on the ship and could see that a lifeboat was being swung out, preparatory to the crew boarding. It was unclear where the black smoke was coming from exactly, but it billowed up and left a pall in the air above.

'What's your course wheelman?' Captain Pearce needed to approach the coaster to enable the lifeboat to come alongside on the port side. The ship was slowing fast.

'266 degrees, Captain.'

'Five degrees starboard helm,' he replied.

'Five degrees starboard helm it is Captain.' This amount of helm whipped the ship's bow to starboard. Seconds afterwards, Captain Pearce, called out.

'Midships.'

'Midships, it is Captain.' At this point Captain Pearce was watching the gyro compass heading relative to the coaster's position.

'Five degrees port helm,' was a followed pronouncement, to steady starboard swing. Shortly afterwards, and once again "midships."

'Steady on 266 degrees quartermaster.' A new course line would establish the coaster on Contessa's port bow and make the ship's gangway accessible. There was no doubt in my mind that Captain Pearce, at this point had control of the situation. I went to the port bridge deck and could see that off watch crew and engineers were on the port side, including passengers. Rapid slow down and severe course alteration left no doubt that something out of the ordinary was afoot. I picked up the binoculars left by Bill, as he answered a call from the engine room. I counted five crew members on the coaster's deck. Two were working to get a boat swung out. Smoke from a hatch at the stern billowed out, but flames weren't visible. I was stood on the port bridge and heard, a creak, creak and another from the aluminium gangway ladder as it was being lowered. I walked back into the wheelhouse and returned, to the bridge wing, with a loud hailer.

'Bosun, Bosun,' I called out. He leant out from the gangway deck and looked up. I followed with 'Station two men on the platform to assist survivors out of the boat and another two farther up, in case assistance is needed.' I received a slow circling hand wave, of acknowledgement, that probably meant that the Bosun was fully aware of what needed doing.

A Slow Ahead instruction from Captain Pearce was followed by "Stop Engines." We were several hundred yards distant from the coaster, when their boat was launched. A plume of blue smoke could be seen from the small lifeboat's stern.

'They can motor across,' said Captain Pearce, 'That makes things easier.' I remember that I walked across the wheel house and into the chart room to refresh my mind as to our position relative to the African coast. The coaster rescue operation having taken us further westwards. At which point, the Radio Officer Paul Reade, burst into the chart room, expecting to find Bill, no doubt. His first words were,

'Captain Peters. Have you taken over? I mean it's an emergency, isn't it? I mean...' I turned from inspecting the chart.

'Do you have, a message, you want to give him?' The

engine was on dead slow and there was relative quiet, in the chart room, when we both heard the voice, recognized, as that of passenger Daniel Musgrove. We, that's Sparks and me were close enough to hear, clearly, his demanding voice.

'These are my people Captain Pearce and we are taking over the ship from now on. Do you understand?' Evidently, Musgrove had entered the Wheelhouse, after walking up the companionway which led to bridge and wheelhouse, accompanied by Helen Taylor. I turned to the Radio Officer, who was wide eyed.

'Is there a Royal Navy presence near Sparks?'

'HMS Exeter's been in contact. Well, not officially, that is.'

'Get a message out to Exeter – "Albany Contessa, under attack, assistance needed"

'What now?'

'Yes, you've got it – go.' I missed Captain Pearce's reaction to Musgrove's question –

'Where's Captain Peters?' It was Bill's response that saved the day.

'He'll be at breakfast, I imagine.' This seemed to satisfy Musgrove, which allowed that window

of opportunity for the radio officer to get a message out.

'Everything will continue as normal,' I heard Musgrove say, before he eventually said,

'Check out the chart room.' Helen Taylor entered the Chart room, with a revolver, held in her right hand, which I recognized as a Beretta. Her first words were,

'Where's the Radio Officer Captain Peters?'

'Most likely at breakfast.' I continued, somewhat courageously, with,

'Where I'd expect you to be.'

'Let's see,' she said. 'Open the door.' She pointed her free hand toward the door, which led into the accommodation area, which included a cabin known as the radio shack.

'I'll follow you to the Radio Office.' There was tension in her voice, but I didn't doubt that she would use the gun on me if I didn't comply. I delayed, by opening the drawer beneath the chart table to insert a chart, which tried her patience.

'Get a move on Captain Peters.'

Once in the corridor, it was with relief that I spotted one of Sparks's Snoppy dog card signs, that he'd drawn, attached to the Radio Shack door handle, with the words – "Gone to Brekkie." I could only hope, that he'd managed to dispatch a morse code message, to HMS Exeter, while having presence of mind to leave for breakfast.

Chapter 15

'Just as I expected,' I said, Sparks is never late for breakfast.'

'He'll not be allowed back to the radio office, except with supervision. We are now in control.'

'What about the owners?'

Yes, Captain Peters, messages will be sent to your company owners. We'll, need time for our manoeuvres and your owners, Captain Peters, will be notified of a temporary breakdown. We intend to project normality throughout this operation.' The quiet demure companion to Daniel Musgrove, was no longer present in this new role. She briefly glanced at her watch, before issuing instructions.

'Go back to the chart room. We can continue this conversation there.' The revolver remained pointed at me throughout. I was not going to rebel or question orders. I opened the chart room door and entered the gloom. Helen Taylor continued with,

'Go on into the wheelhouse.' A wave of the pistol, when I turned, made to ensure compliance. I was greeted by Daniel Musgrove a few feet away.

'Captain Peters, it is good to, have you with us. We have a spare Captain, so to speak.' He pointed a sub machine gun at me. An altogether more lethal weapon than the Beretta held in Helen Taylor's hand. I caught site of Captain Pearce, and Bill Cooper, out on the port bridge. Bewildered eyes of the EDH wheelman darted back and forth. The main engine stopped.

'We continue as normal for as long as possible.' He continued.

'This isn't normal,' I said. 'What are you doing and what do you want Musgrove?'

'The gold, Captain Peters. We are taking five caged pallets of gold. Helen, you have the codes for the pallets?'

'Yes Daniel.'

'How did you get those?' I questioned Musgrove.

'They were in a drawer in Craig Hoopers cabin. Helen made sure we two were busy at cards.

They were easy enough to photograph.'

'But the coaster has signalled distress and in need of crew rescue,' I replied.

'Yes, and we'll have your Radio Officer signal that it has sunk.'

'I don't understand, how you believe you can get away with this.' I answered. It was a still day with the prospect of a blistering sun hitting the decks and accommodation of Albany Contessa. The scream which followed and shouts of 'no, no,' sent a chill through my body, they came from the direction of the gangway two decks down.

'Stay where you are. There seems to be some resistance,' exclaimed Musgrove. I wasn't going to argue. I'd started to walk across to the port side of the Wheelhouse. Musgrove raised his machine gun to waist level. Bill, had made to move toward the port bridge and exit, the wheelhouse, but Musgrove, put a stop to that, barking out,

'You – Mr Cooper stay where you are.' Bill stopped a few feet from the wheelhouse door. Captain Pearce was stood on the port side nearer to the outer-bridge. We were not held in suspense for long. With the engine on stop, there was relative quiet in the wheelhouse and a clatter of footsteps could be heard on the companionway, which led up the port side.

'Mr Mate, Mr Mate.' I didn't immediately see the Bosun when he arrived from the companionway to the bridge. When he got near to the bridge the door, I could see that he was holding a rag to his left upper arm. Evidently, he spotted Bill, inside the wheelhouse and called out,

'They, they – their Captain stabbed me, when, he came aboard. Two of the lads are held hostage. Who are they?'

'Move over Captain Peters,' said Musgrove, 'where I can see you.' I walked to the front by the wheelhouse window spread and joined Captain Pearce and Bill Cooper.

At this point the Bosun saw the machine gun held by Musgrove.

'You bastard.' The Bosun did not spare his words. 'What the hell are you trying to do?'

'Not trying Bosun. Your ship is in our control. I hope you're not badly injured, we will need your knowledge of the ship.'

'To do what?'

'Remove some of the ship's cargo.'

'Bloody highwayman.' I stepped in to diffuse the situation by saying.

'Mr Musgrove, that wound needs attending to.'

'Yes, that is right, Captain Peters. Gentlemen the sea is calm my men are aboard.' The Third Mate had followed the Bosun on to the Bridge.

'And Mr Cooper, it looks like your replacement has arrived,' said Musgrove. 'We require that everything stays ship shape, you might say. Hand the watch over and go for your breakfast. I don't require two Captains on the bridge,' nodding his head back and forth as if communing with some invisible presence.

'One of you can go to breakfast and Mr Cooper.'

'Peters,' Captain Pearce, turned toward me. 'Have the Bosun's wound, dressed, will you?'

'Are we to go unescorted Daniel?' He asked Musgrove. That, Captain Pearce addressed Musgrove by his first name, like some errant school boy spoke volumes about a stoic nature, that would likely place his crews' safety before his own.

'No, Helen will escort you. We can continue with operations. Captain Peters, he turned to address me.

'Mr Cooper and the Bosun I will require to organize hatches to be removed and derricks raised. While Captain

Pearce you will be able to view activities from the dining saloon. Afterwards you will be confined to your cabin, you understand.' I'd removed the green First aid box from the bulkhead.

'That wound needs cleaning,' I pointed toward the Bosun's arm. It was a nasty gash, but the bleeding had stopped. Helen Taylor was now ushering Captain Pearce, First Mate Bill Cooper plus a perplexed Third Mate, through into the chartroom. The Third Mate shortly returned, after presumably being given a very brief update of the ship's position on the chart.

'I'll need to wash and clean the wound.'

'You are not to leave this wheelhouse,' said Musgrove. I turned to the wheelman.

'Can you go to the washstand in the outside corridor – through the chart room?' I ripped open a blue paper package containing cotton wool,

'And dampen half of this. So, it's dripping wet.'

'Yep, Captain Peters. What about the wheel?'

'I'll mind that' interposed the Bosun. 'I've one good arm. Not out of action.'

'All right. Let the Bosun take the wheel and take this to the wash stand,' I handed over the large clump of cotton wool. The wheelman stepped off the plinth and took it

'What is it then?' Queried the Bosun.

'249 degrees Bos.'

The Wheelman walked, with the cotton wool to the nearby chart room door and then to an outer corridor.

At this juncture, two of the supposed rescued crew, arrived on the bridge. One wore a ragged uniform coat of a ship's captain, while the other, was in an oil-stained white boiler suit. The captain's coat jacket was unbuttoned and a holstered revolver could be seen, belted on his left side with a scabbard knife on the other.

'Captain Jenkins, welcome aboard.' Musgrove, greeted them at the bridge door.

'You, said that we'd not meet with resistance, Daniel. Got that wrong didn't you. That one tried to push me off the gangway,' he pointed toward the Bosun, who, in spite of his injury managed a venomous look back. Fortunately, the wheelman returned with the water-soaked cotton wool, at this point and took back the wheel. I grabbed the Bosun's arm.

'This may sting a little.' He winced while I dabbed dried blood from around the wound, before applying a padded dressing.

'Captain Jenkins, let's not cause unnecessary disruption. We've the two most useful people with us to ensure a successful discharge of cargo to African Moonbeam,' said Musgrove. Earlier with binoculars, I'd not been able make out the coasters name apart from Afric – rest of the lettering on the bow was obliterated by rust. More to the point. Albany Contessa, with loss of forward engine power, the ship had begun wallowing in an ungainly way.

'We'll need to head north westerly Mr Musgrove,' I said. 'A course to counter this swell and maintain forward movement, before we warp your vessel alongside.' I was familiar with loading from a barge tied alongside in port. As luck would have it the relative calmness of the Atlantic presented a not dissimilar situation. The Bosun, made a face, as I caused slight pain when I made to tie the ends of the dressing on his left arm.

'You are taking a pragmatic stance, Captain Peters, if I may say. By the by, we'll be taking Craig Hooper with us, once the gold is loaded.'

'Why is that?' I asked, but also, with an appreciation that lining up of the vessels, derricks, opening hatch openings and raising derricks could eat up the morning.

'As surety, as surety Captain Peters. He'll ensure our safe

passage to Cotonou. When Helen returns from breakfast, I will take breakfast and you can manoeuvre into position, for African Moonbeam to berth alongside. We have a curtain of fenders to place overboard. I insisted on this, you see, when we chartered the coaster. I'm not a seafarer, you understand, but I like to run a smooth operation, and would not want to damage Albany Contessa. Your Bosun's injury was, I may say unfortunate, yes, but perhaps it will dissuade others who might hold foolhardy, ideas to offer resistance.' He continued by saying,

'And, please don't try anything on with Helen, Captain Peters. Helen's, a marks woman, with military training and won't hesitate to shoot, where compliance doesn't meet a good standard. I hope you understand.'

Chapter 16

The senior apprentice replaced Bill Cooper's watchkeeping sailor. I sensed Bill's hand in this. Experience from multiple dockings, as wheelman, made this apprentice a good choice to be on the wheel at the time. He would respond well to orders, which would be similar to those given by a pilot when the vessel docked. However, not, in anyway a criticism of the watchkeeping sailors on the Third Mate's eight to twelve watch!

I noted that black smoke, which previously belched from the coaster's stern was no longer visible. In the relative quiet of the wheelhouse the door from the accommodation into the chart room could be heard to open.

'Ah, this will be Helen to takeover while I breakfast,' said Musgrove. Captain Jenkins from African Moonbeam had requisitioned the Aldis lamp and was on the port bridge signalling to the coaster, with his boiler suited companion by his side

Bill Cooper, entered followed by the Radio Officer, then Jane and lastly Helen Taylor. Apart from Musgrove, Helen Taylor and this Captain Jenkins I didn't know whether the others were armed, but later found out that two crew members from African Moonbeam were and provided further protection for the four on the bridge. It also helped to explain how Helen Taylor would have been able to change into a green combat uniform and pick up an AK 47 from between the time of leaving the bridge and this return the wheelhouse, after having breakfasted.

'Daniel, we have not located Craig Hooper. He is not in his cabin.' These were her first words, followed by a jerk of the rifle toward Jane, who was now stood by me.

I've brought Mrs Peters with me to ensure she does not interfere, and is in our sight.' Jane, pulled a face, as if to suggest she did not understand what Helen Taylor meant. Although, caught in a perilous position, I could not fault the logic.

'Passengers and those who are not on watch-keeping duties, are confined to their cabins. There're three sailors on the main deck, Daniel to work deck equipment as we planned.

'Good.' Musgrove turned toward me. 'Captain Peters, you have your wife by your side. Helen will not hesitate to shoot, if she feels you are not following instructions, you'll appreciate.

'Completely,' I said. 'I'm happy to get Contessa ready to discharge into African Moonbeam. The gold is palleted. How many are you wanting?' There was nothing to be gained in obstructing the theft of the gold. This was a carefully planned heist and any resistance would be futile. I was stood in the middle of the wheelhouse and Jane walked across to be with me. Her confident smile belied my actual feeling at the time.

'African Moonbeam we have calculated can take five pallets. A small amount of gold, but of great value to a poor nation like Niger. Right Captain Peters can I have every confidence that you will follow our instructions?'

The safety of the ship and those aboard outweighs all else. I take it you will be leaving us once the gold is loaded aboard African Moonbeam?'

'That's correct. You will be able to continue on course to Lagos.' He turned to Bill Cooper, who Helen had directed to the port side of the wheelhouse.

'Mr Cooper you will go down with the Bosun to the main deck and prepare number one hold for the discharge of these pallets.' Bill and the Bosun, with his arm wound dressed, looked toward me for confirmation.

'Do as he says, I'll alter the ship's course to a north westerly heading of 310 degrees. In the meantime, open up the hatches at number one and get two derricks raised, First Mate, if you please.' These were the instructions I gave to Bill.

'Captain Jenkins,' I called across to where he was on the bridge.

'Signal to African Moonbeam that we're altering course and to keep her distance.'

'Ah,' said Musgrove, 'now I feel confident that with cooperation we can soon have this slight disruption over for you.' Captain Jenkins, if that's who he was interrupted.

'It would be good if we could take that Hooper guy from the bank with us Daniel. We'd have some bargaining power, should anyone be so bold as to intercept our passage to Cotonou.'

'Have your men search every cabin and space. He is somewhere,' said Musgrove who then left for breakfast. I kind of admired the calm and confident way in which he took over. A criminal act without a doubt, but this type of act can be seen as needed, by followers of a political cause, who would argue they have no choices left. I looked toward Helen Taylor who was on the right side of the wheelhouse.

'Carry on as you would normally Captain Peters. Get the ship in position. Your wife can watch her husband at work. I will not hesitate to shoot anyone who is not cooperating.'

'We understand that and I have every intention of getting the ship prepared for discharge to African Moonbeam, without any disruption.'

'Slow ahead Third Mate and wheelman we'll have five degrees starboard helm. The giro repeater gave a course heading of 309 degrees. Shortly afterwards, we started to veer away from the coaster and at 320 degrees I gave the order for midships helm and stopped the bow swing, a momentary five-degree port wheel application, with instructions for the wheelman to steady on 322 degrees.

Soon, the clank, clank made by the rise of the two derricks could be heard and work was in progress to remove tarpaulins and hatches from Number One hold, while dead slow ahead was maintained to steady the ship. With the new course line of 310 achieved, I called out to Captain Jenkins, on the bridge.

'You can bring your vessel alongside now. Have a crewman fore and aft to take a line.' I said to Helen Taylor, 'I need to speak with the First Mate and Bosun.' She replied,

'Don't let me stop you, but do not try anything or I will shoot your wife, you understand.' I picked up the megaphone and walked to the port bridge.

'Have two lines ready to throw to the African Moonbeam.' Both Bill and the Bosun raised their hands in acknowledgement. Their vessel moved in from astern and kept a distance of about fifteen feet, while lines were thrown, to take aboard a warp fore and aft.

While African Moonbeam was being warped alongside Musgrove returned. He placed a brown leather case on the deck near to Helen Taylor.

'Looking good, Captain Peters. Your Captain was very helpful in showing me the layout of the cargo from a cargo plan. It was most interesting to see how the pallets all have strengthened bases and wire attachments, for ease of handling. He said that they were car parts and machinery. It is a strange match that Craig Hooper who is a finance manager, should be responsible for car parts, do you not think? I jokingly asked him if he would use a pallet of car parts as a stake for card playing. It was like an affirmation for me when he said that they were expensive car parts worth ten thousand pounds each. He gave the game away, without realizing, you see, because our embassy already knew that Nigeria was to receive a shipment of ingots and an agent of ours was able to inspect a flat-bed trailer headed for Albany Contessa, to confirm this. I was already certain that the ingots were on board. Number one hold meets my choice for our requirements.'

'For my part, the safety of passengers and crew are first priority,' I said.

'Quite, quite. It is so good that Captain Peters understands the situation,' isn't it Helen?'

'And that neither he nor his wife interfere with our plans, Daniel,' she responded.

'Captain Peters, Helen is not as trusting. She's a trained sniper.' At this point Helen Taylor placed the AK 47 in the corner of the wheelhouse and opened the case Musgrove had brought into the wheelhouse. It was impressive to see the speed with which she assembled the parts of the telescope rifle which it contained.

'Daniel, we will need a pilot ladder to board African Moonbeam to supervise the pallet loading?' Captain Jenkins called out from the bridge.

'I'm sure Captain Peters can arrange that.'

'Yes, but I would like to know where the passengers are?' I stipulated. Jane came in with,

'It's all right Mike, Jackie's arranged a slide show in the passengers' lounge.'

'Yes, they've been told you are offering assistance and supplies to a distressed coaster,' said Helen Taylor as she tightened the barrel of the rifle into place.

'That is all except Craig Hooper,' said Musgrove. 'We have no time to search the ship thoroughly. We will leave without him. Our special operation is otherwise going to plan.'

Chapter 17

I've since reflected on this heist aboard Contessa – what if Captain Pearce had stayed in charge? Unaware that a message attempt had been made to contact the Royal Navy? Would he have put up resistance? Made it difficult for Musgrove and his band of modern pirates to proceed with the gold robbery?

Jane, on witnessing my compliant manner toward Musgrove, had given me a sideways glance, as if to question my attitude. Perhaps, intimating my actions were more that of a coward, than a custodian of a ship's cargo? It was that all our lives were at risk. The Bosun had been knifed. A cold-blooded stare flashed in my direction by Helen Taylor already convinced me that she might feel short changed, if no opportunity arose to show off her marksmanship.

I'll need to hail the Bosun,' I said. 'To get a pilot ladder tied to the railings.

'Go ahead, Captain Peters' Musgrove replied. The bridge phone buzzed.

'Answer it then, Helen Taylor snapped at the Third Mate. I went to pick up the battery-operated loud hailer. Before I could reach the bridge the Third with hand on mouth piece called,

'Captain Peters, the Fourth wants to know how long you want to stay on Dead Slow Ahead?'

'Two hours minimum – if there's a problem let me know – tell him,' I said.

'Two hours sounds good Captain Peters, in my book, said Musgrove.'

'We're fortunate with the sea being flat as a pancake, just now. My men can get the wire caged pallets out of number one, but ... African Moonbeam needs to be able to stow them straightaway.

'Get down there Jenkins,' said Musgrove.' I continued my

walk to the port bridge and directed the loud hailer forward across the windbreak.

'Bosun. Prepare a Pilot ladder for Captain Jenkins to board African Moonbeam.'

I received a raised arm acknowledgement from the Bosun, who was shackling wires from the derricks together, where one was plumbed over the hold and the other over the railings above the coasters main hold. I watched as an AB and EDH went through the mast house door and down into the chambers to take the cargo hook as it descended from deck level. I knew from previous hold inspections that there were five pallets of gold ingots stored in number one. No doubt Musgrove was aware of this after a study of the cargo plans.

I admired the skill of the two ABs who worked the derricks winches. Sat on drivers seats, deft control of winch levers, thrust a wired cargo hook over the deck into the holds centre. The starboard derrick plumbed over Contessa's hold, lifted a pallet out and the other derrick wire dragged it over the ship's railings, to then lower the cargo. With the two derrick wires, like cojoined twins.

The Bosun, in control, like a traffic policeman. With a walk back and forth from hold to ship's side. He gave a downward hand action, to the winchman, who was controlling the derrick above the coaster's hold, Then a stop signal, both vocally and with jerked forward and back motions with the flat of his raised hand. A gentle, descent was made, through a winding hand signal, which stopped abruptly, once the pallet was near settled on the cargo deck of the coaster. Bill Cooper, was leant over the railings, concerned for the ship's forward movement which made the coaster edge slightly away from Contessa's side before being brought back with a creak of sisal ropes, fore and aft.

Paul Reade, Radio Officer, was stood next to the apprentice wheelman, when Musgrove said,

'Is it normal to report a stoppage at sea?'

'Oh yes,' I responded, before Paul could reply. 'Nothing lengthy, just notification that engine repairs are instigated.'

I wasn't sure whether this was true, but awareness of our plight and position, with a signal sent, could register on a British warship's superior radio tracking ability. Anything, that might bring in a Royal Navy presence, to offer protection was worth a try!

Paul, responded with confirmation, by saying that he sent a signal daily and that Captain Pearce would want the ship's position and estimated time of arrival (ETA), sent to Head Office. Astute of Sparks to respond with this, even if it wasn't correct.

'Perhaps, keeping to schedule would be less likely to arise suspicion,' said Musgrove.

'Okay, Helen will escort you, to your station to send this routine message.'

'Lead the way,' she said to Sparks, 'and don't try anything, other than sending position and estimated time of arrival. I won't hesitate to shoot if you disobey. Understand, that my training is in radio signalling. Don't try to send anything different.' She produced the Beretta revolver and left more powerful weapons in the wheelhouse, next to Musgrove, and departed with Paul, for the chart room and then the Radio shack.

I watched, from the outer port side window, of the wheelhouse, as a second, caged gold bullion pallet was first suspended, above number one hold, before it was pulled across and lowered into the coaster's hold, under the Bosun's direction.

'Can't keep course line, Captain Peters,' the call came from the senior apprentice wheelman.

'What's your course quartermaster?' I liked to build up the confidence in apprentices and the title of quartermaster gave confidence and encouragement.

'Three one five,' came back the reply.

'Slow ahead, Third,' I called across to the Third Mate, who was by the starboard telegraph.

'Slow Ahead,' he replied. Steerage would be recovered with extra forward movement, but risked placing strain on the warps, which held the coaster alongside.

'Let me know when you're back on course, Quartermaster.' Within minutes the call came back,

'On course at three ten degrees, Captain Peters.' I reduced speed to dead slow ahead once more.

'It is fortunate with the sea conditions,' said Musgrove, as Helen Taylor returned to the wheelhouse with Sparks.

'I have disabled the transmitter,' she said.

'Good we have only two more pallets to load,' then we will be gone Captain Peters. You understand we wish no one aboard your ship any harm, but our political opposition movement to the existing government, in Niger will have funds to go forward. We will have achieved our objective.'

'There was no need to leave us without a transmitter, was there?' I queried.

'I do not think your ship will sink and when you arrive at Lagos the radio can be repaired. We cannot risk our presence being detected before we get into home waters, you do understand that?'

Chapter 18

I later learnt, from Bill, that the Bosun was all for initiating a response to the theft of the gold. In part, I suspect in that he'd come off worse, after his resistance on the gangway. That all those who boarded, five of the coasters' crewmen, plus the two who joined Musgrove and Helen Taylor on the bridge were armed, quickly alerted everyone to the injury risk involved should anyone attempt to overpower the invaders. I was particularly glad, as was Bill, that apart from the Bosun's failed heroics, no one else wanted to have a go. It was fortunate that Jane managed, after breakfast, to usher the passengers into the lounge for an impromptu talk from Jackie. Bill, made her aware of the ship's takeover, when he left the wheelhouse, for breakfast. Craig Hooper, vanished, it seemed, shortly after the Bosun was attacked. He was seen to watch the coaster's boat from the deck above by the Second Steward. At that point, it appeared that there was a rescue at sea taking place but Bill had the Second Steward tell them,

'Breakfast is only available to those who are in the saloon, within the next five minutes, due to exceptional circumstances of the rescue. A coaster crew man watched the Second Steward, apparently, and was complicit with this. An announcement, which focused passengers' minds, sufficiently to forgo immediate view of the wire caged pallet load.

Questions were asked later, about the discharge of cargo into the coaster, but it wasn't appreciated by passengers fully what had taken place, until stewards brought luggage, which belonged to Daniel Musgrove and Helen Taylor down, to be lowered aboard the coaster. Once the five pallets of machine parts (gold) were loaded, Helen Taylor was first to board African Moonbeam, via the pilot ladder. Telescopic rifle clearly visible slung over her shoulder. Once aboard, she clambered to bridge level and fired two shots above Contessa's main deck. Just clear of those stood on it. Clear warning, that should anyone impede their departure, she wouldn't hesitate to shoot. The coaster's five crew members remained on deck while, Musgrove followed Helen Taylor. Once on the pilot ladder, he could not resist a wave upward to where I was on the port bridge. I didn't wave back, but said to Paul, the Radio Officer,

'Did your message get through to that Royal navy warship?'

'I don't see why not,' he replied. 'I know they've other warships in the South Atlantic.'

It's about steaming time,' I said. 'They might be days away, from where we're positioned, and the shipper will have to say goodbye to five pallets of gold.' The coaster drifted behind and away once the fore and aft warps were released. Out of the blue Sparks said,

'I can fix the radio to transmit, Captain Peters. I've a spare transmitter and receiver in my cabin.'

'Great. Then catch up and see what's happening,' I said. Shortly after the Radio Officer's departure and while Contessa was settling back on to her charted course, Captain Pearce arrived on the bridge, dressed in Captain epauleted shirt and tropical white trousers, which held relevance later, rather than customary shorts. He'd have seen the activity from his cabin window which looked out on deck.

'Five pallets short,' he said. 'Alright Peters, you did the right thing, in the circumstances.'

'Were there any injuries?'

'As far as we know, only the Bosun, sir, as you witnessed. Oh, Craig, has gone missing. They intended to take him as hostage.'

'Yes, that makes sense,' said Captain Pearce, 'I mean from their point of view. He was like the on-board custodian. Poor chap, wouldn't have fancied his chances and now he's gone missing, you say?'

'Well, they couldn't find him.'

'Have the Bosun and the dayworkers go through the ship. He must have found a good hiding place. He's surely still aboard?' I went to the port bridge and hailed the Bosun, to start a search with dayworkers and anyone, who was not on watch or asleep.

The Third Mate, meanwhile, was following the departure of the coaster, with binoculars, when he called out.

'A submarine's surfaced metres away from the coaster.' I grabbed the second pair of binoculars. Sure enough, a cascade of water was falling from the coning tower, above a grey cigar-shaped hull. Before the water was fully clear from the hull, figures, climbed out with rifles or shot guns and as the submarine settled, above the waves, the group, went down to the hull and knelt in a row, with rifles directed toward the coaster. An officer appeared, in the conning tower, megaphone in hand, and with what looked like a heavy rifle slung over his shoulder. The sun picked out a white web strap, before he turned away to face the coaster.

'A submarine's surfaced next to the coaster,' I said to Captain Pearce.

'Were they monitoring what was going on all the time then?' He questioned.

'Looks that way.' I decided not to mention that Sparks got a message away. Anyhow, it could have been that we were unknowingly assigned an escort, bearing in mind the high value cargo aboard.

Sparks rushed into the Wheelhouse.

'Captain,' he was now addressing Captain Pearce.

'I've made contact with a submarine. They've taken charge of African Moonbeam ...'

'And?' Replied Captain Pearce.

'They're ordering it to make for Lagos, sir.'

'Looks like we've not lost those five pallets after all.' Sparks, unaware that we'd already viewed the submarine surfacing, I said,

'Further good news, Sparks, we can see the submarine from here,' I said and passed the binoculars across to Paul.

'My pal on Exeter must have got the message,' he said as he got to focus on submarine and coaster.

'A nuclear sub apprehending a coaster with rifles and small arms. Not a sight you see every day,' he remarked. Captain Pearce questioned my previous response.

'You did get a message out then?'

'Well, yes, that's me and Sparks were in the Chart Room. We both heard Musgrove take over with his arrival the Bridge. It was touch and go, but I stalled Helen Taylor when she wanted me to go to the Radio shack, and stop messages getting away. Sparks, evidently did get a message away. The Snoopy – "Gone to brekkies," was pretty neat Paul,' I said.

'I'll need to get a message to Head Office Mr Reade,' said Captain Pearce. Come with me.'

It was gone midday, but undaunted, by the disruption, the Second Mate had worked out a dead reckoning which allowed for the time we departed from Contessa's course line, distance steamed and appropriate course adjustment needed to re-join the proper course. A sun azimuth caught from the boat deck, would give a reasonably accurate position, since an early morning sextant altitude had been taken by him also from the deck below. Apparently, a crewman from the African Moonbeam was detailed off, by the coaster's captain to watch and stand guard, as the Second took a sight.

The heist, apart from the skirmish with the Bosun, was followed through with calculated minimum disruption. A bit like a shop lifter who will claim that he only takes enough for his needs from large retail store groups, which can afford to write off losses, rather than small shop owners. As if theft from large organizations is somehow not really a crime. This, in the thief's mind somehow justifies thousands of pounds of shoplifting over time. Of, course this was a significant theft and on a grander scale than shop lifting. The Third Mate had gone below and effectively, the watch was now in the capable hands of the Second. It was well past midday. A Second Mate's bridge watch keeping covered from 12 to 4pm. I was able to leave the bridge. A sense of normality having been reclaimed. Captain Pearce made no comment about his insurrection with cabin confinement, but no doubt was not best pleased about losing command.

Chapter 19

'How exciting,' said Jacqueline Braithwaite, as we walked away from a late lunch in the Dining Saloon. Bill Cooper apparently interrupted the lecture given in the passenger lounge to say that the ship was being relieved of part of its cargo. He decided to explain that it was a heist organized by Daniel Musgrove and Helen Taylor. This was Jacqueline's response, to us, that's Jane and me. She wasn't that concerned for the Bosun, either.

'He's a bully always has a go at the junior sailors and he punishes them by cutting short their "smokos." I've timed him between calling "Smoko," and getting them back to work.' Smokos, consisted of two breaks; one mid-morning and the other in the afternoon, where the dayworkers could lay down paint brushes, scrapers, chipping hammers or maybe break from overhauling and greasing wires and derrick blocks to have a hot drink and maybe a ciggie, for ten to fifteen minutes. Jacqueline could have been right, but it was not my place to call out the Bosun, where he came under the First Mate's area of responsibility

'Jane, you were on the bridge where the action was. It can be incorporated in one of my talks.' She continued.

'I'm not sure the shipping company would approve, Jackie,' replied Jane, who thought up a good reply before I could. But I added,

'No, there's a special cargo which belongs to the government aboard.' I didn't mention that it was gold ingots.

'It comes under the official secrets act.'

'That's a shame. There goes a basis for a good novel.' We smiled and Jane said,

'See you in the lounge for the Beetle Drive this evening, then Jackie.' Jane like me was keen to have some down time from ship and passengers. I opened our cabin door. We were not released that easily.

'You'll be out for our regular afternoon foursome deck golf match Jane? Must keep our lives on stream. Shame Helen will no longer be available to play. I'll miss that.'

'Yes Jackie, we should continue as normal. I'm sure Mike will recommend that.' I smiled encouragingly.

'Didn't know your friend Jackie held such strong views about the Bosun,' I said, once inside our cabin.

'Nor did I Mike. Looks like he'd have got a spot of detention and have to write lines if he were in Jackie's class.

"I must treat young crew members with more respect," or similar. We were sat on the day bed talking about inconsequential things, in the way that you do, to offset events that have been traumatic and life threatening.

'Foreman's can often come in for stick. If they look as if they're easy-going. British crews can be great in a crisis but not always that enthusiastic on the work front. A Bosun needs to show he's boss.'

'But in a fair way.'

'We all have good and bad points. I'd like to have Bill's version about how things are.

I explained to Jane how Paul Reade had managed to get a call out for assistance.

'But it didn't stop them getting away with five pallets, did it,' she said.

And causing distress to everybody aboard.'

'It was lucky that we were out of sight in the chartroom otherwise he wouldn't have been able to nip and get the message out.' I then explained lead up events to Jane.

'Sorry Mike, but it's all too de'je'vu for me. You do see that?'

'Of course.' I'd been all too casual about what Jane had experienced

'Mike, I just remember that look in Pepe's eyes when he

held me hostage on Albany Princess. Daniel Musgrove had that self-same look. Revolutionary zeal, whatever it is that drives them blazes out of their eyes. You just know that lives are at peril, because they care nothing for their own; save that of furthering their cause and you realize that lives lost have no consequence.'

'Are you sure you're alright?' A double tap on the door followed. It was Peter Haynes.

'How's everyone? Didn't see that one coming.' His face popped into sight as the door opened.

'Come on in Peter,' I said.

'Poor Jane, it's like a revisit from Albany Empress days.' Peter walked across the cabin and sat in an easy chair opposite to where we were.

'How are the other passengers taking it Peter?' She asked.

'They'll be alright. Great idea to batten them down with one of Jacqueline Braitwaite's talks. Not sure Captain Pearce's a happy man, though. Are you doing a tour of the ship?

Mike?' Peter sort of jumped the gun, but Jane followed up with,

'I think you should Mike. Perhaps it might be a good idea if the two of us meet and greet with crew and passengers, to give assurance that –

'Part of the cargo's been stolen, but otherwise everything's okay?' said Peter.

'Well, not exactly,' said Jane.

'They didn't get away with it,' I said.

'How's that Mike, five pallets left the hold to my reckoning?'

'Ah, but the Royal Navy intercepted them, before we lost sight.'

'You saw this?'

'Yep. Paul managed to get a signal out to HMS Exeter.'

'And the ship just steamed up and aimed its guns?'

'No, better than that. A navy sub surfaced right next door

to the coaster. Both Bill and me saw this. With binoculars, that is. The coaster's being escorted to Lagos. The pallets will reach their destination.'

'Who else knows about this?'

'Captain Pearce and the whole ship shortly, now I've told you Peter.'

'Hey Mike, you make me out to be a gossip.'

'Come on you two,' said Jane. A clatter was heard outside, before a call of "Captain Peters, are you there?" and a hammer on the door. I got to my feet and opened the door.

Chapter 20

The Bosun, with a fresh dressing on his stabbed arm, was on the other side, of the open door.

'Captain Peters, there you are sir. Mr Cooper sends his regards. We've found the passenger Mr Hooper, sir. Not in a good way, that is. Well, he's dead sir. It looks like frozen, sir. We found in him in Number two chilled compartment.'

'Where's Mr Cooper Bosun?'

'At number two.'

'Has Captain Pearce been informed?'

'I'm on my way, but your cabin was nearest and Mr Cooper is wanting to know what to do with the body.' Chief Steward Peter Haynes called out.

'It might be as well to leave the body where it is if it's in a chiller compartment. Until we reach Lagos, that is.' In a matter of fact, way he continued with,

'We can have the body stitched in canvas and then it'll be ready to be hoisted out on arrival.'

'Right,' I said.

'This is terrible,' said Jane. 'Poor Craig.'

'Bosun, you'd best carry on to the Bridge and inform Captain Pearce that Mr Craig Hooper has been found. Got that? And pass on the Chief Steward's recommendation.'

'Yes sir, I'll do that right away,' and he was gone.

'Peter, we'll go to Number Two and get Bill Cooper to organize a canvas body bag. I've a spare duffle coat and woolly hat.'

I'll fetch it,' Jane said and got up, walked over to the double wardrobe, opened it and grabbed woollen hats from the top shelf and hooked down a duffle coat to hand to Peter and another for me. It was all very matter of fact, but after the trauma experienced, this information didn't seem to measure very high in the stakes, at the time.

Once out on the foredeck, we met up with Bill, First Mate, who opened the mast head door, for us to meet with chilly hand rails and steps which led down into the refrigerated chamber.

Craig Hooper's body was lay against the wall of the empty chilled hold. His contorted face didn't suggest an easy death.

'Doctor Sinclair could perhaps give advice,' I mentioned to Bill.

'I was thinking along those lines. Poor fella, he could've picked any other hold and the temperature might have allowed him to survive the cold. The engineers were chilling the hold to make ready for a first cargo of mangoes at Lagos.'

'Or was that why he chose this hold to hide in? We shall probably never know, but he obviously had no intention of falling into the hands of Musgrove and his crew.'

'Do you want me to ask Doctor Sinclair if he'd take a look?' asked Peter, Chief Steward.

'I'll clear it with the old man first Chief, I said. Leave the body as it is for now. We returned to the warmth of the main deck and I made for the Bridge, entering through the port side.

Captain Pearce lowered binoculars, from his eyes and turned toward me.

'I never felt comfortable about Musgrove. My suspicions were proven right. We've lost Craig, Peters. He was a worried young man and now we can see why.'

'Do you think he knew that Musgrove was after the gold Captain Pearce?'

'He was concerned at the lack of supervision. That news might get out that we were carrying an extreme cargo of gold. He told me he was more worried that a foreign power might know about the cargo. He wasn't totally reassured, when I said that we could call in protection from the Royal Navy. NATO exercises are in progress, but he said that short of an armed escort there was, he felt no real protection.' He paused to have another scan of the horizon with the binoculars.

'I don't understand politics, to any extent, Peters, but apparently gold can purchase arms and supplies without the limitations of paper money. They speak of oil being the new gold.

What did stagger me though, was when he told me that we have on board the largest consignment of gold to be shipped, in peace time between countries.'

'The five pallets have been recovered, though,' I said.

'Yes, Young Paul Reade did well to get that message out. That coaster's under escort to Lagos.' Bob Mitchel, Second Mate, poked his head out from the chart room.

'We're back on course, Captain Pearce. ETA's five hours later than before, but The Senior Second said he can increase revs, if you want?'

'No, no tell him to maintain one hundred, arrival's not time critical. Burning extra oil to gain a few hours won't achieve anything with this contract.' I asked Captain Pearce about an inspection of the body.

'Chief Steward Haynes suggested that we might get Dr Robert Sinclair to look at the body. He seems to think it's best that it stays where it is.'

'Yes, Dr Sinclair, is a medical doctor. Send my regards Peters, and tell him that I would be appreciative if he gave his opinion. That's if he's happy to clamber down the ladders.'

It was mid-afternoon and tea was being served in the passengers' lounge, when I found Doctor and Mrs Sinclair sat in the far corner.

'Tea, for you Captain Peters?' Asked the steward as I entered. "Yes." I turned to Dr Sinclair and his wife,

'That's if you don't mind my joining you.'

'Of course, do join us, Captain Peters. I grabbed a spare chair from another table and sat down with them.

'Then poor Craig. Whatever happened? How did he end up in that chiller compartment?'

'That's where we hope your husband can be of assistance. I know nothing about medical matters other than out of a St John's ambulance First Aid manual.

'Dr Sinclair,' I looked directly toward, where he was sat.

'Captain Pearce has asked if you could bring your experience to bear, regarding Craig. I mean we assumed that he froze to death in the chiller hold, but how does the face react?

Craig's face is contorted. Is that normal doctor?'

'Could be, but short of doing an autopsy, not sure that the cause of death can be easily established, precisely. I'll certainly take a look. I do have pathology background training.

What are the plans for the body?'

'Chief Haynes has suggested to leave it in the chiller compartment until we arrive at Lagos. He has past experience in these matters.'

'Yes, that chilled compartment is probably as good as anywhere. You have togs that I can wear down there and good lighting?'

'Certainly Dr Sinclair. It's very good of you to bring your professional expertise to the situation.

Chapter 21

Captain Pearce, was in the wheelhouse with the Second Mate, when I returned.

'Dr Sinclair's being taken down number two to have a look at the body, sir.

He's not sure about whether he'll be able deduce anything, but has a pathologist training background.'

'Good, good said Captain Pearce. Paul, the Radio Officer, was stood at his elbow, with a typed message

'Just received this from Head Office Captain.'

'Another enquiry about our ETA, no doubt?'

'No Captain, it's about one of the passengers. You need to read it.' Paul returned to his radio Shack. I was about to leave, but was called back.

'Listen to this Peters,' and he read the message just received.

"The body of John Palmerston-Smyth has been discovered in the basement at Blue Circle Line Head Office by our boiler engineer, which means that the passenger registered aboard Albany Contessa is an imposter. The authorities in Lagos are now placed on stand-by to question afore-mentioned imposter passenger on arrival at Lagos. We have been advised that you do not question his authenticity and continue to treat said person, in as bona fide person of Mr Palmerston-Smyth."

'What does this mean? What's going on here?' said Captain Pearce. 'Hold your horses, there's more.'

"Informed of incident of theft, but relieved that Royal Navy has retrieved loss.

Company, is very concerned over the tragic death of Mr Craig Hooper.

Next of kin will be visited by personnel to convey message of distressing news.

Arrangements are in hand to fly the body back to the UK with assistance from agent and Nigerian authorities. A special bonus for ship's company, in light of extra-ordinary demands placed on crew is being considered by the company."

'No mention of the Bosun and the ordeal everyone has been put through. Typical of head office to be so matter of fact. But...' We were on the starboard side of the wheelhouse and were unaware of the presence of this person, we knew as John Palmerston-Smyth at the port bridge door opening. The wheelman was first to notice him, from his raised position on the plinth abaft the ship's wheel.

'Captain Pearce,' he called out. I looked across and sunlight glinted from a silver revolver held authoritatively across the imposter John Palmerston-Smyth's jacket.

Evidently, he'd heard the message read out.

'Yes, Captain the message is correct. I have been chosen to take over the ship and direct it toward our ships, which will take over the remainder of the cargo. It was a useful diversion to have Mr Daniel Musgrove take your navy away from the scene, for the small amount taken.'

'And who are you?' Captain Pearce asked, as he walked on to the matting of the Wheelhouse. Now with the revolver pointed towards us.

'Captain Pearce I am Major Nikolai Dimitrijevic of the USSR. The gold you have on board is to be requisitioned for our future use. It was unfortunate, but Mr Craig Hooper got caught in the cross fire and had to be eliminated. I have a course to take your ship away from the coast and toward one of our escorted ships which will relieve you of the remainder of the gold. It was a useful diversion that Musgrove tied up your Royal Navy.

There will be no signal from or to the ship during this period. We have blocked airways, temporarily. But I would have you call the Radio Officer away from his office and into the wheelhouse, immediately Captain Pearce.'

'Second Mate, get him in here would you,' he said to the

Second Mate. The wheel position obscured the two of them from Dimitrijevic, but Captain Pearce pointed to the deck and at his white deck shoe which was unlaced. The Second Mate responded by saying,

'Captain Pearce your shoe is unlaced, you could trip.' It was one of those random incidents that seemed out of context, to the extent that Dimitrijevic did not respond with a threat to not move. Captain Pearce you could say was well prepared. He placed his foot on the wheelman's plinth and appeared to be tying the right shoe lace, while he took hold of a revolver holstered on his right leg. I did not know then, that he belonged to a Liverpool shooting club. The crack from the pistol was deafening in the relative confined space of the wheelhouse. Dimitrijevic was hit in the face. Blood splattered the near wheel house window as he was thrown back and instantly killed.

'I decided to be prepared this time,' said Captain Pearce. The wheelman was the least astounded by what happened.

'Great shot, Captain,' he said, whilst he altered the wheel position by several spokes to maintain the ship's course.

'Second Mate,' Captain Pearce turned to address him.

'Yes Captain,' he replied.

'Call the engine room and say that I require maximum speed until our arrival, into Nigerian territorial waters.

'Yes, sir.'

'We need to get there as soon as possible. His body,' Captain Pearce pointed with the pistol toward Dimitrijevic.

'He can be stitched in canvas and join poor Craig, in number two's chiller compartment.

Peters. I must see Sparks to update head office of developments.'

Right, Captain Pearce, I'll get it organized.'

With that, he left the wheelhouse to work with Radio Officer Paul Reade on a message for Head Office.

The wheelman had completed his hour on the wheel and I took the opportunity, at the changeover to get him to contact Chief Steward Haynes, together with the Bosun, to organize disposal of this Russian major's body. A clatter of footsteps up the companionway on the portside heralded the arrival of the Third Mate, with Doctor Sinclair following. I stepped over Dimitrijevic's body, which straddled the bridge doorway.

'Third Mate there's been another attack. You can see Captain Pearce for-stalled it with the ship's pistol.

'Really, Captain Peters? It looks like the gunfight at the OK Corral.'

'No need for an autopsy with that one,' said Doctor Sinclair who was now knelt over the body.

'What about Craig Hooper, Doctor Sinclair?' I asked.

'Quite straightforward.' He looked up from where he was examining the bullet wound to the head.

'I took a sample of saliva and it was laced with strychnine. And who is this – threatening the ship's safety...?'

'Yes, he was bidding his time. A major in the KGB,'

'Not, then the actual Mr John Palmerston Smyth?'

'Doctor Sinclair, Captain Pearce was notified by head office that the real Palmerston Smyth was found dead in the basement. He was about to take the ship to the Soviets, but unbeknown to us Captain Pearce was armed with a ship's pistol,' 'And a crack shot at the shooting range in Liverpool,' chimed in the Second Mate.'

'Yes, I can see,' replied Doctor Sinclair.

Chapter 22

I met Bill Cooper on my way to inform Captain Pearce that Craig Hooper was in fact poisoned. The First Mate was making his way to take over the four to eight-watch.

He would have known about the attack in the wheelhouse, from the Second Mate's wheelman, who'd witnessed it and had given Bill his wake-up call.

Bill wasn't into an afternoon nap, but a customary call fifteen minutes before, gave an awareness of the approach of his four-to-eight, wheel house watch. He stopped and said,

'Who was it this time? Jack told me that Captain Pearce saved the day. Who'd have believed he was up to downing an attacker, like that?'

'A Major Nikolai Dimitrijevic of the USSR, apparently. Paul Reade brought a message that stated the real John Palmerston Smyth's body was found in the basement of head office.'

'Really? But then I always thought there was something fishy about the guy.

Bill, the ship's still vulnerable from attack by the Soviets until we reach Nigerian waters.

Yes, and he must have poisoned Craig Hooper.

'How do you know that?'

'That's it! Doctor Sinclair found traces of strychnine in his saliva. And Dimitrijevic said Craig was in the way. Anyhow, I'm off to update Captain Pearce about the poisoning. Craig was sort of caught in the crossfire, but Musgrove unwittingly helped the soviets by creating a diversion for the Royal Navy.'

'And the body?'

'It's joining Craig's in Number Two.'

'Everything's back to normal then? Like??

'Keep your eyes peeled for Russian warships. May not have the Royal navy around to look out for us, with Musgrove and crew, creating a distraction.'

I let Bill go, to take over the watch and before entering, tapped on Captain Pearce's door He was sat at his coffee table, with what looked like a glass of whisky.

'Come on in Captain Peters.' For some reason I'd regained my position of Captain and not just Peters.

'Shook me up that did, you know. I just visualized his face as the target at the shooting club.'

'You got the bulls eye Captain Pearce.'

'How do I stand? I mean, never killed a man before, you know.'

'Don't worry you were defending the ship from attack. We'll all be behind you.'

'That's reassuring.'

'Captain Pearce, Doctor Sinclair has confirmed that Craig Hooper died from strychnine poisoning. He detected the presence of the substance in his saliva.'

It confirms, really what Dimitrijevic, said. He didn't want Craig taken as a hostage and poisoned him.'

'And put him in Number two hold, to make it look like suicide,' said Captain Pearce.'

'It does look like that.'

'Head Office have been informed and they're contacting the foreign office. Musgrove was seen as just a robber on the high seas. Now that the soviets are involved it's taken everything to another level.

'Peters,' my elevation to Captain had not lasted for long.

'You must get out and about with your wife and reassure the passengers, officers and lower deck that we'll soon be in Nigerian territorial waters and safe from any further attacks. I don't know how true that is, but we'd best run with that.'

'You're alright sir?' I asked.

'Why wouldn't I be. Just worried that killing a soviet major might lead to a diplomatic incident.'

'We'll support you, don't worry. The ship had already been held-up by Musgrove with an attack on the Bosun. It was done in self-protection for the whole ship's company and passengers, in my book.'

'Thank you, Peters. Musgrove, what happened to him? I'll not feel the ship is safe until we're tied up in Lagos. Never believe I'd say that about the place.'

Chapter 23

I went away, in awe and admiration for Captain Pearce's ability to adapt to the threat, by arming himself – and for his pistol shooting skill, but also with an appreciation that his short-term memory, was muddled, if anything, perhaps worse than when we set out. He must have seen Musgrove leave on the coaster? Maybe, his focus on the bridge hold-up, triggered, his response to return to the bridge armed. I certainly couldn't have taken, a ship's pistol in my hand and been sure of hitting someone ten feet away, never mind fifteen. Certainly, not with a direct hit to the head. I later learned that his target practice shoots had been with the self-same pistol. A duplicate one, to that held aboard Contessa. Protective and restraining items aboard cargo liners consisted of a strait jacket, hand cuffs and a ship's pistol.

Cabin doors were unlocked once more. The response to the first attack by Musgrove had been to treat this, as an in-port situation where both passengers and crew were instructed to lock cabin doors.

On opening my cabin door, I found Jane having tea with Chief Steward Peter Haynes and Jacqueline Braithwaite.

'What happened on the bridge this time Mike? I mean we know Palmerston Smyth's been shot,' asked Jane, the moment that I'd closed the door.

'Some explaining to do. Can I have a cup of tea first?' A cup and saucer remained on the tray. I sat next to Jane on the day bed, while Peter and Jacqueline Braithwaite, were sat opposite in wicker chairs, which were more suited to deck rather than cabin use. They creaked when sat on, together with the motion of the ship and whenever either of them moved, which was a bit disconcerting. Peter got to his feet and set up the cup and saucer.

He poured the tea and added milk, before he placed cup

and saucer in front of me, and sat down.

'Fire away Mike.'

'Right.' I decided to edit the account and not mention the true identity of Mr John Palmerston Smyth.

'This time we were held up by Palmerston-Smyth. The long and the short of it is that, the Old Man had made provision against another attack and had a pistol holster attached to his ankle, and shot Palmerston-Smyth, who in fact was an imposter.

'Was he badly wounded, Mike?' Asked Jane. I mean did he shoot him in the arm or leg?

'Face,' I replied.

'Yippee do,' exclaimed Peter. 'No messing about there, but he's a top marksman at the Liverpool shooting club.'

'You know about that then,' I said. 'He was killed instantly.'

'Never liked the man,' said Jacqueline. 'He said my talks were too low brow and would not be attending.' I wasn't of the opinion that that was a good enough reason for the shooting, but it was a way, no doubt, for her to deal with the direness of the situation.

'I'm supporting the captain, in his actions. I don't feel that I can go into further details,' although the crowd (crew) would no doubt have been given a highly descriptive account by Jack, the wheelman on watch at the time.

'Captain Pearce wants us to visit remaining passengers and crew to reassure them that everything is back to normal,' I reached out and placed my arm around Jane.

'Alright by me, she replied.

'The passengers will be in the passenger lounge after dinner and I'll notify off duty officer watchkeepers to be there. I can get the message out that they should attend, said Chief Steward Peter Haynes.

'That will be a good time to explain and reassure everyone,' I said.

'Looks like I've got the plot for a crime novel, from events so far,' said Jaqueline 'So much excitement.'

'I wouldn't classify these two events as excitement. Everyone has been at risk. The second attack could have been even more severe than Musgrove's, had Captain Pearce not have for-stalled it,' I said.

Chapter 24

We visited the galley first and Chief Cook Brian Steele was not at all surprised that Captain Pearce shot the soviet major.

'Sailed with Dougie Pearce for past twenty years. He'd not let a soviet agent take the ship over. Crack shot with a pistol. Did you know that, Captain Peters?'

'I do now,' I said.

'Crew from the coaster, with that Musgrove passenger, smelt the baking bread and we fed them a breakfast. Said the coaster's cook was no good and would I board their ship and cook for them. I made some excuse that we'd a first-class galley and could only cook with good ovens. They cleared off, luckily, to make sure everyone stayed in their cabins.'

'Sounds like a good move on your part Chief to offer them breakfast.'

'Don't think they were over committed to the cause, you might say, but this soviet one sounded as if he mightn't have been concerned about anyone on board, particularly.'

'Sure, you could be right, Chief,' said Jane. 'I've really enjoyed meals on board. It's not just a rest from cooking for me, I couldn't produce meals to such a good standard ashore, let alone aboard a ship in bad weather.'

'Thank you, Mrs Peters, it's kind of you to say so.'

'Not at all.'

'As ever,' I said, 'very well-fed, but not so well paid.'

'You should be so lucky, having such a good Chief Cook,' said Jane. Worried, perhaps that he might be the reason behind some domestic upset, Chief Cook Steele, said,

'It's good of you and Mrs Peters to come and see us, sir, but better get back to see that the galley boys not sneaked off for a ciggie.'

The Bosun had the dayworkers back on greasing and overhauling wires and derrick blocks. We bumped into the

Electrician, who had taken the back off number one winch, to check it out, after the unload of the pallets into the coaster.

'If I'd known they were going to take part of the cargo out of number one, I'd have made sure the winches were out of action and under repair.'

'Probably worked out for the best Leckie,' I said. We got rid of them. The bigger threat was from the soviets.'

'He was a Major in the Russian army, wasn't he? Not from Head Office, at all.'

'That's right. The real John Palmerston-Smyth, that's his body, was discovered in Head Office's basement. A message came through just as the soviet imposter arrived on the bridge. The game was up for him.'

'Was he armed, then?'

'Yes, but Captain Pearce wasn't allowing another hold up and shot him dead.'

'Captain Pearce comes across as a bit of a James Bond figure himself.'

'He did the right thing in my book. The Major was about to take the ship to the soviet fleet.'

'Why would that be?' I wasn't sure whether he already knew about the cargo of gold. The cases loaded on to the coaster contained gold, but were marked up as machine parts.'

'Perhaps they were short of rations?' I suggested. He seemed to settle for that answer, but asked,

'Where are the soviets now?' I pointed across and over the port side.

'Out there somewhere.'

'Coming after us?'

'Hopefully, no. We're hot footing it into Nigerian territorial waters, where we'll seek protection from their navy.'

'It's still all a bit hairy then – Captain Pearce, and a ship's pistol are no match for a Russian warship.'

'That's true Leckie,' I replied.

Without risk of getting into further conversation with other members of the ship's company, we left the main deck and climbed the companion ways, to the door which led into the passengers' lounge.

Chief Steward Peter Haynes had assembled the remaining passengers in the lounge and was offering refreshments from the bar.

The moment that we entered through the lounge door, both Paul Jensen and Stewart Hopkins walked across to confront me. I thanked my lucky stars that Jane was with me or their attitude might have been all the more aggressive and mine to theirs.

'Captain Peters,' it was Paul Jensen who button-holed me first.

'Are we right in thinking that the cargo is something other than machine parts and manufactured items stowed in boxes.'

'Yes,' said Hopkins. 'Why would a revolutionary force that Musgrove supported want
a cargo of machine parts?'

'Unless of course those boxes contained armaments? Queried Paul Jensen.'

'And how did a soviet major come to be aboard the ship?'

'That I don't know,' I said, but let me into the room first, and I'll do my best to answer your questions.'

I decided not to openly reveal that part of the cargo, was gold ingots packaged within crates, which were boxed and labelled, to denote agricultural machine parts, among other categories. They seemed to go along, in part, with a third world argument, where machinery and equipment would be highly valued in the case of Niger and Musgrove's hold-up, but were not convinced about the soviet attack.

'There's something the soviets wanted and it wasn't just the ship, was it Captain Peters?' Paul Jensen insisted.

'The cargo does not belong to Blue Circle Line. We aim

to deliver the goods assigned to their destination port. The shipper pays a charge to the company. It is a business contract. Potentially amongst three parties. The owner of the goods, the shipper and shipping company. I was back pedalling, but knew that it was better that these two were kept in the dark.

'The situation of the soviet hold-up will be a matter for the British and Russian embassies on our arrival at Lagos. I cannot reveal any more Mr Jensen. Our main objective is to get Albany Contessa into Nigerian territorial waters for the protection and safety of yourselves, the ship's company and the cargo we carry.' I could tell they were not satisfied with my answers. Doctor Sinclair understood far more about the true nature of events, but remained quiet, save for the end when he asked.

'When, is the ship due to arrive now, Captain Peters?'

'Let's see,' I said, 'It's Wednesday. ETA is now set for Friday afternoon. We are at maximum speed to make up on some lost time.'

'We don't mind if the ship's a little late, do we Lucy?'

'No, we can have a final deciding match, on whose, the champion deck golfer.'

Chapter 25

As can happen, when events occur which are not easily explained; there can be a certain flippancy of approach by those involved. The medical profession, when on the doorstep of life and death patient care, probably needs to wind down tension and create a relaxed attitude, rather than dwell on basically, events that have been distressful, but cannot be changed. Doctor Sinclair and his wife's attitude, was an antidote to the stress and anxiety which had built up aboard Contessa in the past twenty-four hours.

After the evening meal on that Wednesday in July, I left Jane with Jackie Braithwaite who had organized a scrabble match between engineering officers, deck apprentices and passengers in the passenger lounge and made for the bridge. Bill Cooper was near to the end of his watch and was hoping to get a few evening star azimuths for Second Mate Bob Mitchel to work on during his watch (12 to 4). Good star sight with about six azimuths would give Bob an opportunity to pin point Albany Contessa's position within a quarter of a mile. On land this might not seem very accurate, but in the vastness of the southern Atlantic this was a good result.

Before the arrival of GPS, celestial navigation with altitudes taken of sun and stars in combination with current almanac reading for star positions was by sextant. During sunrise and sunset, where stars and horizon were visible, this was the most accurate method of ship position finding, deep sea, when out of range from shore-based radio signals. The ship's chronometer accuracy monitored with a daily Greenwich radio signal and a measurement taken from a ship's log of distance run between sights enabled trigono-metric calculation to reinterpret a position in the heavens to the sea surface. Spherical curvature envisioned in the night sky translated back on to the earth's curvature, where the actual ship was positioned within a six-bearing configuration of the stars, moon or planets targeted for their altitudes at a given time. Land based compass bearings from the ship required a minimum of, three, ideally well spread location bearings, to then give a pinpoint intersection, pencilled, hopefully, spot on, to the chart course line. Regular fifteen-minute checks enabled the officer of the watch to access whether the ship was clinging to its course line, otherwise a degree or two-adjustment, would be needed. Tidal drift might necessitate a charted course of 265 degrees, for example to be 267 degrees, to bite into the tidal pressure and maintain a sought, actual course of 265. Star altitudes, mimicked the land triangulation bearing process with spherical trigonometric calculations made to take the celestial imagined ship's position, from the heavens, down to the sea surface, and on or close to the charted course, the ship was following

I waited while Bill dashed from bridge to chart room. Once, the Third Mate had taken over the watch and Bill would be later free to talk.

I leant over the bridge windbreak. A warm breeze was refreshing, after the heat of the day sun. Phospherescence, within the bow wave was starting to emit its spangled sparkle, when Bill came across to chat.

'Saved the day, didn't he? Those days spent at the shooting range, it seems prepared Dougie for this very situation,' Bill said, when he arrived to where I was leant over the bridge.

'Don't know what the authorities will make of it,' I said. 'You can't just go around shooting people you don't like.' I was taking the view of devil's advocate, in suggesting a worse case, scenario.

'It wasn't like that Mike and you know it. Look He'd been locked in his cabin while the Bosun had been slashed with a knife and will have watched Musgrove steal five pallets of cargo and to top it all, armed crew members from the coaster maraud the ship, scaring the living daylights out of us all. He took the view that it wasn't going to happen again on his watch, excuse the pun.'

'I understand what you're saying Bill, but in that instance, with Musgrove, it was more like shop lifting. Major Dimitrijevic was, to my way of thinking, acting in the soviet union's interest, and that makes it political. If he'd succeeded, in taking all the gold, then there would have been an almighty political row. It's all on a knife edge between Russia and the west. The soviets maybe could point to Britain's past where Elizabethan privateers plundered Spanish galleons and took the plunder back to their queen, from their action. But seriously, it's very much an international incident. We'll have to wait and see how it makes out once we're in Lagos' I said.

'How's Dougie?' Asked Bill. 'You've been seeing more of him than me. I mean memory wise?'

'Episodic, might be a good way of putting it,' I replied. 'He seemed to relate to a bigger picture. I mean he grasped, in a way that no one else did that the ship could still be vulnerable to attack. He'd strapped the pistol in a holster around his ankle and as we know was prepared to use it. It was only when I mentioned Musgrove. He seemed to have lost recall of what happened.'

'How do you mean Mike?'

'Well, he asked me about what happened to Musgrove. He was, it seems aware of the bridge attack but not that Musgrove and Helen Taylor, departed in the coaster. I mean his window looks out on to the foredeck. He would have seen the pallets being discharged in to the coaster.'

'Could he have fallen asleep.'

'Do you really think so?'

'No, I don't Mike. But then how will it run that he shot and killed Dimitrijevic?'

'In his favour, if I have anything to do with it.'

Chapter 26

Earlier, Jane mentioned that Captain Pearce could be forgetful. Apparently, he'd asked whether we had any children, even after explaining that they'd been left with their grand-parents, when we first met. He made out that he'd momentarily forgotten. I did explain that this trip to Lagos was his final one, but not that the company had charged me with keeping watch on his actions while on the bridge. Not, that is, until I met up with Jane, after I left the bridge, that Wednesday evening as we approached Lagos.

'You should have told me.'

'I just saw it as in the line of work.' She was sat on a chair with a towel wrapped around her head, while smoothing her nails with an emery board. I'd made coffee for the two of us and was measuring a teaspoon of condensed milk to stir into my coffee. Jane made a decision to have black coffee when there was only condensed available, once away from shore supply of fresh.

'I can see that it was a compassionate thing to do, but I'm not sure the shipping authorities would see it that way. How would it work out if it was known an airline pilot had memory loss and it was said that the co-pilot could step in if the plane was not being piloted in a safe manner. They'd have said that the pilot should have been ordered to step down, and replaced. Wouldn't they? Wouldn't they Mike? I mean did Blue Circle Line know about his memory lapses Mike?'

'They knew and Bill knows, but Captain Pearce is married to a cousin of the owners and this will be his last trip to sea as a ship's Captain. I guess it's exceptional.'

'Would you have been given overall command if Captain Pearce was retired on health grounds, then?'

'Probably not.'

'There you are. You're a good company's man, Mike, but...

'Look Jane, it's understood by Bill how it is.'

'And Tim Burroughs, the previous Staff Captain, before he became ill? Did he know?'

'Yes.'

'Don't you see that's probably what made him ill. That burden of responsibility.'

Although, I didn't like having myself corrected at the time. I realized that Jane was right.

'Yes, but he didn't have a wife on board to confide in and give him support.'

'That's true. Think yourself lucky Mike Peters.' I walked gingerly across with the tray of coffee, as the cabin deck moved downwards, in response to the pitching motion of Contessa's bow, plunging through Atlantic rollers, now with maximum propellor revs to speed our journey to Lagos.

'Thanks Mike,' she said, as I placed her black coffee on the table. I sat in the adjoining chair.

'Am I forgiven?' I asked.

'Yes, because I know my husband and it's in your nature Mike to help others. But I do wish you'd told me about Captain Pearce from the start. I mean, how responsible are you for the ship? I know if Captain Pearce fell seriously ill, you'd take over as ship's master, and on the bridge. going in and out of port the captain, has overall responsibility. Isn't that a bit risky with Captain Pearce? What I'm trying to say – is he cognitively capable of following what's going on?'

'Put bluntly, not always. There is a risk, that he might not pick up on error in a pilot's instruction.'

That's where I have to be on the bridge, going in and out of port where a situation could become critical.'

'You were in the wheelhouse when Captain Pearce shot that soviet agent?'

'Yes, but no one could see that coming, Jane.'

'How will things look then, if it comes out that Contessa's

Captain has memory lapses?'

'Not good I grant you, but hey, that's in the future.'

'And you've got to make sure Albany Contessa docks safely in Lagos. Even if it means countermanding Captain Pearce's orders?'

'I'm hoping it won't come to that Jane. But I have backing from Blue Circle Line that the company will support my taking over, if Captain Pearce is not understanding or failing to interpret necessary manoeuvres with the pilot on board.'

I'm kind of married to a potential modern-day Fletcher Christian, then?'

'I wouldn't put it like that Jane.'

'Isn't it mutiny when another officer disobeys or fails to respect the authority of a ship's Captain?'

'Yes Jane, but I can verify authority from head office.'

'Like waving a magic wand and saying abracadbra and suddenly Captain Pearce disappears. It all sounds like a very risky position that you've placed yourself in Mike!!'

Chapter 27

On Thursday morning the outer door which led from the port boat deck into the accommodation slammed shut and shortly afterwards, there was a repeated tapping on our cabin door. It must have been about forty minutes after breakfast. Jane and the passengers were on the starboard side getting in a game of deck golf.

I opened the door and a bronzed EDH from the Third Mate's watch, dressed in jeans, tee shirt and flip flops was standing outside.

'Morning Captain Peters. The Third sent me to say that we're near to entering Nigerian territorial waters.'

'Right, I replied. 'And Captain Pearce?'

'He's on the bridge sir. Should I be telling the Third that you're on your way?'

'You can do. Thanks for the call.' He turned and walked back to the outer door.

I'd met the Third outside the dining saloon earlier and let it be known that I required a call. I estimated from yesterday's noon Day's Run position that it would be about ten o'clock, when we would be close to Nigerian Territorial waters. It was ten past ten when I left my cabin and walked across to mount the companionway which led from boat deck to bridge. Before I entered the wheelhouse, I saw the telegraph move outside from full ahead to Stand By on order of Captain Pearce. A tanker, low in the water passed by well clear on the portside. Captain Pearce would have entered Lagos many times before and now with an experienced pilot, there should be no problems.

'There you are,' Captain Pearce came across from checking the giro heading. It was never questioned why I appeared on the bridge at critical times such as port entry. Tim Burroughs, similarly will have been tasked to be present at these times.

Perhaps, the Captain was aware of his memory slippage and valued our attendance. This was his last trip before retirement and there would be questions asked about how two passengers came to be killed once we tied up alongside. It was an anxious time.

The Nigerian Navy are sending an escort to watch over our progress,' he said. Bit late now that we're in their territorial waters anyhow.' I scanned the horizon ahead with binoculars, and spotted a sleek vessel twenty degrees on the port bow, in battleship grey.

'There's a naval vessel twenty degrees on the port bow. I handed the binoculars over to Captain Pearce, just as Paul Reade, Radio Officer walked across from the chart room with a typed message for the captain.

'Just made contact with Nigerian navy Captain Pearce.' Captain Pearce handed back the binoculars and read out the message.

"Welcome to Nigeria. We are watching over your safe passage into Lagos."

Captain NNS Aradu.

I looked again at the ship. It was a modern vessel. A guided missile ship. A significant presence in these waters.

Very shortly after this we took on a pilot and tugs guided Albany Contessa alongside, where armoured vehicles were stationed at either end of the dock. Customs clearance took over an hour, but in that time an armed guard was stationed both on the ship and by the gangway.

I was with Bill Cooper, who was supervising the sequence of unloading with the stevedore manager on the gangway deck, when Paul Jensen came out of the accommodation.

'I knew that this ship wasn't carrying an ordinary cargo,' were his words to me.

'I'm still not at liberty to disclose what we are carrying. Only that our main cargo back to the UK will be mangoes.'

'I'll take this up with the company. After all we've been through.'

'You may have to do that Mr Jensen. We've been given customs with quarantine clearance. You may wish to take a break ashore.' There was no way of denying that the cargo was of importance with the military protection given to both ship and cargo, but I had no intention of advertising the fact that the protection was for high value gold ingots. To ensure that they reached bank vaults without being stolen.

It was a tense situation, but he realized that I was not going to discuss the cargo contents with him and went back into the accommodation.

I noticed that a Mercedes car had arrived near to the dock, since we'd been given clearance, but did not attach any significance to this, before the Second Steward came down the companionway from the deck above.

'Captain Pearce wants to see you Captain Peters,' he said.

'Where is he Second? I asked.

'In his cabin. There's a visit due from the British Embassy. Will it be about the shooting?'

'I don't know. You already know more than I do,' I said, which was true. I'd not known that we were due a visit, so soon.

'Could that be them?' He pointed towards a group of two men and a woman who were nearing the gangway below. I went down on the main deck to inform Bill Cooper as to who they might be.

'I'll check them out Mike. If they're from the embassy, and escort them up.'

'Can you leave the Second Mate to manage deck proceedings, Bill?'

'You want me to join the tea party in Duggie's cabin then.'

'Yes, I do,' I said.

Chapter 28

There was obviously going to be investigations into the death of two passengers aboard Contessa. I was curious as to who we were going to meet. I knocked on Captain Pearce's door. Chief Steward Peter Haynes opened the door, which was then left open.

'Bill's greeting what looks like a delegation, and showing them up, I said.'

'Come on in. I'm setting up some refreshments.' The passenger and senior officers steward was with him. I noted that Doctor Robert Sinclair was sat in an easy chair.

'Angie, you've got those flags to pin on the sandwich triangles?

'Those that say marmite and cheese and Heinz sandwich spread? Yes, Chief.'

'That's a bit ordinary,' I said.

'They love home ingredients Brits posted overseas. You wait and see.'

'Haynes, this isn't a vicarage tea party,' said Captain Pearce, who was looking across from a window, which faced on to the foredeck. A table clothed trestle table was set up against a bulkhead with cups, saucers, milk, sugar, tea spoons, two coffee pots, and side plates, at one end with covered plates of sandwiches and Macvities chocolate biscuits at the other.

'You said no alcohol, Captain Pearce.'

'We're not entertaining customs or foreign dignitaries, that's right. They'll have to return to their offices afterwards.' He paused.

'You've probably got it right Chief.'

'We'll cover the sandwiches and biscuits with a cloth, Captain. Mind the cups and saucers when you remove it.' This remark was directed toward me, as Angie unfolded a white table cloth to cover mainly the sandwiches.

133

Footsteps and voices could be heard approaching. Chief Steward Haynes went to greet the approaching embassy, representatives, while Angie left the cabin to return to passenger duties.

Captain Pearce and myself were in white tropical uniform. I was dressed in white shorts, knee length socks and black shoes, whereas he wore tropical white trousers. Both of us with the four banded gold epaulettes on our shirt shoulders, which denoted Captain. He picked up his gold oak, leafed white cap from the coffee table and placed it under his left arm. There was no mistaking which of us held the more senior rank. I was stood to the right of Captain Pearce.

'I've asked First Mate, Bill Cooper to join us,' I said.

'Sensible move Peters. That makes one more of us.' I wasn't sure how Captain Pearce might react, and this reassured me. Doctor Sinclair got to his feet, as the party approached.

Chief Steward Haynes walked in, and turned to the first British embassy representative to enter.

'First secretary may I introduce you to Captain Pearce.'

'Welcome aboard First secretary.' Captain Pearce replaced his cap back on the table before stepping forward. The First Secretary introduced himself.

'Charles Williams, Captain Pearce. Pleased to meet you.' They shook hands.

'I wish we were not meeting in such sad times captain, where two of your passengers have lost their lives. I have with me Tristan Dewberry and Jill Downing part of my support team.' Bill walked across to where I was stood. Captain Pearce replied,

'My Staff Captain Peters,' he briefly moved a hand in my direction 'and Doctor Sinclair, is with me who volunteered his expertise, while travelling as a passenger. You've already met my First Officer. Please have a seat.' Extra chairs had been placed around a coffee table, which fronted a three-seater sofa. The support team, who were with Charles Williams sat on the sofa, where he chose, an easy chair, which was probably where Captain Pearce would have chosen to sit. The chair had its back to a front cabin window and allowed light to flow directly onto proceedings. Two mahogany chairs, more suitable for deck use were on the far side. We that's myself and Bill Cooper sat on these, while Captain Pearce commandeered the easy chair opposite to where the First Secretary sat. There was no doubt who was going to chair this visit. Charles Williams, opened his brief case and removed a dark blue folder, with HM Government, in white across its front with heraldic design. The two on the sofa held notebooks with pens, at the ready to record the session, which was how it seemed to be developing into.

'Gentlemen, or perhaps officers and gentleman, would be more appropriate.' He referred to Doctor Sinclair who had chosen a seat by the window, initially, until I walked across to assist his carrying of the easy chair nearer to where we were gathered. Doctor Sinclair was now sat to the right of First Secretary Charles Williams.

'I need to make clear that an attack aboard a British merchant ship by a foreign power constitutes an attack on the sovereignty of the United Kingdom, and is a contravention of international maritime law. While he announced this Charles Williams opened the folder and removed A4 pages, held together with treasury tags. He held the document in his right hand.

'This is a transcript of a document which we received from the British Foreign Office, two days ago, through the services of MI6, and effectively defines their understanding of events. Knowledge, they have about the attackers. A Mr Daniel Musgrove and partner Helen Taylor and most recently a certain Major Dimitrijevic, who we understand was shot and killed by you Captain Pearce?'

'Yes.' Captain Pearce answered from his position opposite.

'It was not my intention to kill him,' which registered with me as untrue, 'but one of my crewmen had been attacked previously. The man held a revolver in close proximity to others within the ship's wheelhouse. I instinctively,'

'Fired to kill, can I say?'

'It turned out that way. I don't regret the shooting of this Dimitrijevic fella. It was not just the cargo. It was the prospect of,'

'Being captured or worse by the soviets.'

'That's so.'

'And you are – an experienced revolver marksman? No, there's no need to answer. Passengers and crew were blessed to have you there in the wheelhouse at that moment, Captain Pearce,' said Charles Williams. He paused for a moment.

'Whatever is discussed and revealed in this cabin of yours Captain Pearce, remains here. Is that understood?' His eyes moved around the room to encompass us all.

'Nothing that concerns this visit is to be revealed to anyone. This matter, is within the domain of state secrecy, in order to secure the safety of the British nation, commonwealth and dominions. I'm here, you understand, to reveal the outcome of HM Government deliberations over the matter of these two attacks on,' he momentarily, looked inside the file, your ship, Albany Contessa.'

He turned toward Jill Downing. A member of his support team, and said,

'Jill, you have additional copies of the transcript with you. Would you be so good as to hand them, out?' These copies cannot be retained, you appreciate, but I propose to read the document to you and any questions anyone has we will attempt to answer. This is a ruling at most senior government level. You will be able to ask questions, but you must understand that this is the action to be implemented and not a document to debate about or in any way alter. It is a summation that has been made to accommodate the tensions at present that exist between western government and soviet Russia. You may not agree with the action proposed, but is a resolution that the government believes best serves the interests of national security.

Jill, when you're ready please' We, that's Captain Pearce, myself and Bill Cooper now held a copy of the transcript in our hands.

"On Thursday July 26th, 1984 the department was informed that a Mr John Palmerston-Smyth died of strychnine poisoning. His body was discovered in the basement of Blue Circle Line offices, Liverpool. Information, that became critical when their passenger list for Albany Contessa included this person.

Blue Circle Line had apparently organized a sabbatical for John Palmerston-Smyth which, in part comprised a voyage to Lagos aboard aforementioned vessel. The company knew that his name was registered on the passenger list and their awareness was that he joined the vessel and was indeed aboard the vessel on passage to Lagos.

Captain Pearce, master of Albany Contessa was messaged immediately by his company to be instructed that the passenger purporting to be this John Palmerston-Smyth was an imposter. Instructions were given to maintain the deception and not confront this person. That the authorities in Lagos would arrest or apprehend this bogus passenger, in due course.

The department at this point were unaware that Albany Contessa two days previously had been held up by two passengers, while going to the rescue of a distressed coaster. These passengers were later named by the company, as Mr Daniel Musgrove and Miss Helen Taylor.

Investigations subsequently made have established that

Daniel Musgrove of Nigerian descent was a leading member of a revolutionary group who planned to overturn the governing body in Niger.

Albany Contessa, at the time of the first hold-up was, twenty miles westward of Accra, Ghana. The distressed coaster had sent a false Mayday signal and the crew, when rescued over ran the ship and, at gunpoint, made Albany Contessa's discharge five pallets, marked as machine parts to the Coaster's main hold.

Blue Circle Line have disclosed that bulk value of Albany Contessa's cargo outward bound has been gold ingots, disguised with outward, packaging which denoted machine parts.

It has been revealed that Miss Helen Taylor was a former employee associated with the transhipment aboard Albany Contessa and that partner Daniel Musgrove made arrangement to stage a fake Mayday alert by the coaster. A sizeable amount, five pallets, were discharged into the coaster's main hold, but a signal to HMS Exeter enabled a submarine to surface nearby and escort it, with the gold into Lagos. Both Mr Daniel Musgrove and Miss Helen Taylor were aboard the coaster."

'Hold it there Jill, a moment please.' Charles Willliams called out and she stopped reading.

'Is there anything, so far, that you gentlemen would not agree is a realistic account of events aboard, yes, your ship, prior to a further attack which led to the fatal shooting of Major Dimitrijevic. This being, albeit, a much-abbreviated summary?'

Chapter 29

'This is all very well,' said Captain Pearce, but in Number two hold two bodies are stowed in canvas bags. One, as far as I can see was an innocent victim. You could say, passenger, Craig Hooper was in the wrong place at the wrong time. The other held up the ship and looks to be involved in the murder of John Palmerston-Smyth.'

'Captain Pearce, you understand that there are issues here that transcend everyday events. Britain and western democracies are in a cold war situation with Russia and cannot allow an escalation into a combat zone which could mutually destroy both sides should open war escalate. Investigations have been made. You appreciate. The Russian embassy in London, have been in correspondence with our Foreign Office and now in turn the Foreign Office have directed our embassy in Lagos, whom I represent on how we are to act. The transcript we have here is in effect the ruling laid down and which is to be implemented. I can take it that you concur with events described so far?'

'In a very abbreviated recall, as you mentioned,' I replied.

'Right, thank you both Captain Pearce and Captain Peters.' A sort of Tweedledum and Tweedledee reference to our input. It was apparent, to myself at any rate that a fait-accompli was in place, regardless of any input from the three of us.

'Shall we let Jill continue? to see what has been decided and how procedures are to be followed?' This was a rhetorical question on the part of Charles Williams, First Secretary from the British Embassy, Lagos, in that the British state or maybe the western alliance itself, in the form of NATO, would have decided on the approach and resolution to be brought to the matter.

'Thank you, First secretary.' She continued.

"An intervention by the British Royal Navy was timely and apart from a knife wound inflicted on the ship's bosun by a crewman from the coaster's boarding party, no other physical injuries were sustained to passengers or crew members. Albany Contessa returned to its course line, on passage to Lagos.

Radio Officer Mr Paul Reade, instrumental in making contact with HM navy immediately following on from the first attack received a message from Blue Circle Line, that the body of Mr John Palmerston-Smyth had been discovered in the basement of their offices."

'One moment Jill,' Charles Williams intervened.

'The message you sent back, Captain Pearce, was that "you read the message out loud," in the wheelhouse?'

'Yes, I did. No argument with that, is there?' Replied, Captain Pearce.

'No, no just verifying. Please continue Jill. Thank you.'

"Believed perpetrator. A Major Dimitrijevic, was in the bridge area and heard the message being read out. He previously managed to disguise his person, in adopting passenger status of the real John Palmerston-Smyth.

Although, this Major Dimitrijevic was himself armed with a revolver a distraction created by Captain Pearce gave an opportunity to remove a ship's pistol, holstered to his right ankle, covered by tropical trousers and to shoot Major Dimitrijevic, fatally in the head. It needs to be noted that Captain Pearce is himself a highly skilled pistol marksman. Verification has been made, by the Liverpool Pistol Association, of which he is a member. In their words,

"Captain Pearce would be unlikely to not hit Major Dimitrijevic in the head, as target, with his skill attainment."

Following, on from the previous hold up, passenger Craig Hooper could not be found aboard. Craig Hooper was placed aboard Albany Contessa by his company to accompany their cargo, which was that of gold ingots to its final destination –

the Bank of Nigeria. Daniel Musgrove's intention was to take Craig Hooper hostage aboard the coaster, apparently, but it appeared that he had managed to evade prospective captors. Blue Circle Line's information and messages via Albany Contessa to the company have enabled this analysis.

His body was discovered by the Bosun, in Number Two hold, which was on test for its chilled effectiveness to take a cargo of mangoes. Doctor Robert Sinclair, a passenger aboard the ship, with background pathology training agreed to examine the body of Craig Hooper which later revealed that there was strychnine in his saliva. The same method of assassination inflicted on the actual Mr John Palmerston-Smyth, who was found in the basement of the Blue Circle Line offices. Only relative, that is to John Palmerston-Smyth, is a sister who lives in Australia, according to Blue Circle Line sources.

The department will contact her, but it has been decided that his death will be attributed to natural causes. That of a heart attack. The same cause of death is to be attributed to Mr Craig Hooper. It is the opinion of the department that this will alleviate unnecessary distress to families, friends or relatives of the two deceased. It is also vital not to destabilise relationships with the Soviet Union further.

Correspondence, at ambassador level with the Russians has revealed that they believe this Major Dimitrijevic is a member of splinter group, which threatens the Russian state and that his actions are not in any way countenanced by the USSR. The Foreign Office wishes, to make it clear that they have no reason not to trust this explanation given, by the Russians. The body of this purported Major Dimitrijevic will be collected, through the auspices of the Lagos Russian Embassy. A hearse will be dispatched and once the body is secure inside the coffin – at present, in a chilled compartment aboard Albany Contessa, will be discharged by crane discharged by crane to their awaiting hearse.

141

Our – British Embassy, will supply two coffins and hearses. One for the body of Mr Craig Hooper and the other to indicate that John Palmerston-Smyth was aboard. The empty and occupied coffin both to be flown to the UK.

It is to be reported that both passengers, unfortunately died aboard Albany Contessa and arrangements will be in place to dispatch the coffin, already indicated to be that of John Palmerston-Smyth, the deceased, to the mortuary where his body will be kept in refrigerated conditions and placed in the coffin. His sister will then be notified on his unfortunate passing, while aboard Albany Contessa, near to the port of Lagos. Similarly, for Mr Craig Hooper's body. His actual body, in this instance will be flown back to the UK, with close relatives notified of a fatal heart attack aboard the vessel.

Two innocent civilians have been placed in front of a runaway vehicle, which can be named political greed. There is no dispute that in both instances criminal and illegal actions catapulted these two British citizens, namely Mr John Palmerston-Smyth and Mr Craig Hooper into the face of tragic outcomes, namely their death.

This plan has been prepared at the highest level for implementation. Mr Charles Williams, First Secretary for British Embassy, Lagos, Nigeria will notify senior officers aboard Vessel Albany Contessa of this ruling, with understanding that these events aboard the vessel, in the interests of national security are never to be revealed to anyone." There was a pause. Jill Downing looked up from reading.

'Thank you, Jill, for that,' said Charles Williams. While she collected the transcripts from us, I asked.

'How does this resolve questions asked by the crew, First Secretary, about Major Dimitrijevic. A Wheelman was present when Captain Pearce shot Dimitrijevic. He will have related what happened below decks, and throughout the ship's company?'

'Thank you for bringing that up, Captain Peters. The message to be given out is that all information about the attacks is now in the control of MI6 and investigations are being rigorously pursued. You can stress that no further information can be made available, due to ongoing threat to national security and that similarly to directions I have given you any further talk on board or on arrival back in the UK would likely place British lives at risk.

'So much for everyone's equal under the law,' exclaimed Captain Pearce.'

'Some, more equal than others, perhaps?' said Bill Cooper.

'These are exceptional circumstances and do you want to be arrested for manslaughter Captain Pearce?' Replied Charles Williams.

'The Russian Embassy, on direction from the Chairman of the Politburo have informed our Foreign Office that this Major is effectively a renegade. And as stated before, the Foreign Office see no reason to distrust their pronouncement. However, under British law a man has been killed and this would normally warrant a civil police investigation.'

I intervened.

'Don't necessarily buy the Russian story. The fact is Mr Williams, Captain, passengers and crew had already been subjected to what amounts to a brutal attack. I considered the hold up, by what to all intent appeared to be a Russian agent as a greater threat to the safety of all on board and fully support Captain Pearce's actions.'

'Thank you for offering your view, Captain Peter's. I'm sure Captain Pearce will value your loyalty, but the fact remains that a civil police investigation has been halted by intervention from MI6 following on from this ruling and decision from the Foreign Office. I admire and respect your duty of responsibility and care for those aboard Albany Contessa, but I think you both should see that an amicable resolution with the Russians is very positive, in light of the tinder box nature of the relationship between the two super powers.

At this point, Captain Pearce got to his feet.

'Perhaps, you three would care for some refreshment. I certainly would.' We, that's Bill Cooper and myself walked across to the refreshment table, and removed the cloth which covered the sandwiches.

'That's good of you Captain Pearce.' Bill, stood behind the table and handed out plates. True to form, as Chief Steward Peter Haynes had predicted that there was recommendation for the sandwiches.

'Marmite. I miss that, said Jill Downing. That's great, when she saw the flag – "marmite and cheese." atop the triangular sandwiches.

'Can't stand the stuff,' said Tristan Dewberry, who had been observer and recorder throughout the visit.

'But do like sandwich spread. Remind me of school sports days. We were given sandwich spread sandwiches afterwards.'

'Chocolate biscuits tick my box,' said Charles Williams, who went on to fill his plate with them.

Chapter 30

There was little delay in the removal of the two bodies from number two hold. Two hearses arrived in the dock area, shortly after the delegation from the British Embassy left the ship. Coffins were lowered into the then open number two hold and hoisted from ship to shore with the bodies inside. The hold was the first hold that would cargo load chilled mangoes.

The coffins, once ashore were laid on trolleys and wheeled to the waiting hearses. Number three hold was already discharging pallets of marked boxed "machine parts," on to a curtain sided lorry dockside. The armed guard stationed by the lorry reminded me of the armed guard experienced when alongside in communist Poland. The lorry cab, liveried with the words engineering and machine specialist. A hoax that was followed through at this end, but the armoured cars and soldier presence suggested that something valuable was in need of protection.

I was on the boat deck with Jane, watching proceedings.

'You'd not have expected armoured cars at the dock,' she said.

'There could be something political going on, we don't know about,' I said. That was untrue but plausible. I knew what was going on, but not in a position to discuss the situation with Jane.

'Did the British Embassy arrange the removal of the bodies?' She asked. I was able to answer that question.

'Yes, in collaboration with the Russian. I don't believe either want to pursue matters further.'

'That's incredible! And how long do we have in port do you reckon Mike?

'Possibly – ten days, depending on the load rate of the chilled cargo. There can be delays. in hot weather with hatches open. A rise in temperature can occur in the cold chamber below deck with the influx from the outer warm air. Loading, has to stop. Hatches covered to bring the temperature down.'

Guided tours around Lagos were organized for the seven remaining passengers and the shipping agent provided a car, which was available to drive senior officers and passengers into the city centre.

It was the Friday after the first weekend that the ship was fully loaded with a main cargo of chilled mangoes. A pilot, familiar with both the ship and Captain Pearce boarded late afternoon. Lines were released from the dock and tugs at the bow and stern, took charge to swing Albany Contessa, out of the dock and back into the open seas

A quiet sea passage, followed, until the ship reached thirty north and Albany Contessa began to pitch and ship water over the bow, shortly afterwards. The skies remained overcast, as I remember, until we approached Liverpool and a brilliant red sunrise, appeared when anchoring to await a pilot.

Unbeknown to Captain Pearce head office had booked outside caterers to board and set up a buffet in the dining saloon, once the ship was cleared by customs. After the crew signed off in the mess room, those who'd sailed under Captain Pearce for a number of years were invited to a farewell party. Apart from a few of the officers in uniform, civilian clothed office staff and ship's crew made up the main body of the party celebrating. Doctor Robert Sinclair and his wife attended, as did Jacqueline Braithwaite who qualified as having been a regular passenger when Captain Pearce was master.

Champagne corks popped and Captain Pearce, who, enquired off me earlier, whether I thought the British police might be waiting for him, was in a relaxed mood, when it was discovered, this was not the case. I was also, at that time, I remember adamant that I did not drink more than two fluted glasses of champagne, although Jane disagreed.

A taxi for the two of us was booked for nine thirty to take us home to 19, Hanover Gardens, Liverpool. Both looking forward to be back with twins Dinah and Carol who we'd left with Jane's parents Paul and Natalia Anderson. Suitcases and grips were taken to the bottom of the gangway. Laughter and talk could be heard from the party still in progress, after all the cases were taken ashore. I went back aboard for a single lightweight holdall. The gangway was not the ship's own, but railings had been removed from the main deck and a roped wooden one, with wooden slatted treads rolled across from quay to deck. A gradient down from the main deck to the dock.

I remember, that I slipped and fell down the ramp-like gangway, with a searing pain in my left leg, but not much else. I was knocked unconscious from bumping my head on a bollard. I was told about this later and that my leg caught on a wire spring.

When next I opened my eyes, I was in a hospital bed with a nurse leant over.

'You've badly damaged your leg from a fall Mr Peters.' I must have been given pain killers, since there was a numbness rather than pain coming from my leg and I felt a drowsy sensation.

'What day is it?' I asked.

'Saturday,' she said. 'And you're at the Royal Liverpool, awaiting further treatment.'

'I only remember slipping on a gangway.'

'That was Friday.'

'And I've been out all that time.'

'Never mind, your wife and family will be here this evening to see you.'

'Nurse Barnes,' a strident voice called from further up the ward.

'You need to attend to Mr Palmer. He needs assistance out of bed.'

It was the ward sister, I presumed.

'I'll be back,' she said. 'You must stay in bed for now.'

My left leg badly lacerated and broken from being caught on a wire, from ship to shore, although it did prevent a fall into the dock itself!

Epilogue

The visit by the store to see Diana Ross was deemed a great success. That was not only by the store management and staff, but also Dinah and Carol, who were at an age where parents can be seen as an embarrassment. It was great that they felt able to be with their parents that evening.

It was Jane, who encouraged me to look to a future, which did not entail months away from the UK. The twins even seemed to have grown since we'd been away, at the time of our, return from Lagos, Nigeria. My leg accident on disembarking, was attributed to the champagne by Jane, but which I denied.

When I became homesick as it were for being aboard a ship, it was recalled by Jane that her father trained and worked as a pilot, before we met. That maybe I could return to a sea-going occupation, once the twins were through school.

But that was for the future. Sale posters had arrived for the Autumn sale plus "sale," purchase lines, which needed to be worked into various departments.

The End

Other Books by Sam Grant

Please check out these other publications by Sam Grant.
Follow blogs, poems and stories at
Samgrantpublications.wordpress.com
Sam Grant, Author – Facebook.

Atlantic Hijack (978-1-78222-291-0)
Action, mystery
Sea adventure in the South Atlantic
A secure orderly passage aboard a cargo liner is Ripped apart by a brutal terrorist attack. Author Sam Grant brings his professional seafaring experience to Bear in this thriller that sounds all too familiar from Our evening news bulletins. Apprentice Mike Peters is finding his feet amongst a cast of nautical characters as the Albany Princess voyages to Montevideo. But the ship's personnel are not all that they make themselves out to be as revealed during a rapidly unravelling hijack in the South Atlantic.

River Escape (978-1-68222-574-4)
Sequel to *Atlantic Hijack.*
Action, mystery,
Venezuela: An oil terminal in the River Orinoco, Venezuela. Following on from a military coup. Mike's pressured efforts to prepare the tanker for the load of boiler oil – compromised by a refinery postponement.
An influential young woman, boards who starts calling, the shots? Hidden identity of a rescued yachtsman and two female companions further compromises the ship's safety ...

Dancing on the Beach (978-1-78222-431-0)
Romantic thriller
Phillip Norton obtains summer work as a deckchair attendant

in Batcombe. Previously he works at a bank in the City. Part of Phil's duties are to deliver dairy cool boxes to the Sea View Hotel via the cliff railway. Soon he is into a heady romance with the receptionist. But with cruise liners anchored off Batcombe Bay the Sea View not only hosts holidaymakers, but also has connections with a more sinister trade...

Persuasion's Price (978-1-78222-687-1)
Mystery thriller
A quiet market town in England is shattered by an explosive mix of gang rivalry and shady deals. A family is torn apart and, with the involvement of the secret services, events take an unexpected and sinister turn.

Persuasion's Price
The Play (978-1-78222-870-7)
Play, in ten acts. Includes full script and stage instructions ready for rehearsal. Drama group requires curtained stage.
Back stage management has six-scene preparation.
Cast of thirty-two, with possible, actor duplication for smaller parts.
Ninety minutes run time, plus interval.
Brief Summary:
Believed to be hidden in quiet market town away from prying eyes. Anton, son of a Russian family is confronted by secret service. Discovery of illegal smuggling, leads to deal being struck.
Meanwhile, an overseas ransom is offered for kidnap of farmer's daughter.

Galactic Mission (978-1 78222-512-6)
Science fiction
It is 2110. In an advanced technological world of holograms transmitted by mobile phones; food made by a Maxi Maker,

drone trays, clones and automata concierges, QUADRANT is the world government. But the world is not at ease and relationships are put under strain. James Walters is a sales manager for an international conglomerate, based in the UK. One day he encounters Adriana – "The Empress Adriana" – from the Galactic Command Force ...oh, and ruler of planet Earth and all Planets Force, with help from some Inspiring sources thwart planetary conflict.

Galactic Mission Part Two (978-1-78222-773-1
Science fiction, sequel to Galactic Mission
In this classic sci-fi adventure, the main characters from Galactic Mission, including the Empress Adriana, are working to divert comets away from Earth by firing a missile from Mars.

Adriana, has decided to stay in human form, but seeks a closer relation-ship with James, who prefers Lara. He backs away. Adriana is restricted in power. Although Captain Dryson and Alfredo – two android machines – carry out her instructions. After the comets are directed away from earth, Galactic Force returns with Antar-XP200, and two new androids, to replace Adriana, on Mars.

Adriana regains full power and a chosen group leaves for earth by spaceship with the intention of gaining control over Quadrant, who are returning, now that earth has been saved.

Poetry and short story publications by Sam Grant

Poems with themed notes (978-1-78222-464-8)
Love Starved by Electronics is a sonnet selected for a 'Sonnets for Shakespeare' anthology.
In *Riding Through Time* ghostly horsemen appear to ride down the ages.

Captured into their Realm – a meeting with an alien depicted in verse.

Eye of the Storm; The Time Makers Kingdom; Thankful Thoughts and *Spirit of Spring*. These are a few of the poems in this varied anthology.

Notes have been prepared and included by Sam Grant to give background information and set the poems in context.

Mists of Time (978-1-78222-708-3)

From epic poem to scary short story, *Mists of Time* entertains and enlightens. In the title poem, author Sam Grant takes us on a journey. Perhaps his journey, down a leafy lane to a farm in summer, off to sea and beyond.

Secret Cave is a short story informed by a love of sail boat sailing, a reflection from the author's young life, before the author embarked on a career in the Merchant Service.

Part One – Poems both in traditional and modern form.
Dramatic, but also light-hearted topics explored.

Part Two – Short stories.
Individual cameo chapters.

Sam Grant, Author

URL *amazon.com/author/grantsam*

samgrantpublications.wordpress.com

Books are available from good bookshops. Please give ISBN
Online site, Book Depository, also lists Sam Grant novels with
delivery worldwide.